I0547493

Justice for *Julia*

Healing the Wounded Heart series

Book 2

By Donna Schlachter

(c) 2021

ISBN: 978-1-943688-82-1

Published by: PLS Bookworks, Denver, Colorado

Where Publishing Dreams Become Reality

Note from the Author

All characters are from my imagination. Medical malpractice was a common charge women doctors faced in an effort to expel them from their vocation. As this story takes place in 1868, the Civil War is but a few years in the past. During this conflict, tens of thousands of soldiers died on the operating table or from infection, and many more tens of thousands were maimed for life.

The Female Medical College of Pennsylvania did exist at the time, graduating fully-trained women doctors who faced many uphill battles to be accepted by their male colleagues.

References to medical practices are historically accurate.

All scripture references are from the King James Version of the Holy Bible (KJV)

Books By Leeann Betts:

By the Numbers series featuring Carly Turnquist, forensic accountant

Mysterious Ink Bookstore **series**

featuring Margie Hanson, librarian

The Game is Afoot

Little Grey Cells

Heavier than Broken Hearts

Counting the Days: a 31-day devotional

In Search of Christmas Past – a novel

Always a Wedding Planner Romance Collection

(Barbour Publishing June 2021)

By Leeann and Donna:

Nuggets of Writing Gold -- articles and essays on writing.

More Nuggets of Writing Gold – more articles and essays on writing

Books by Donna Schlachter:

Mended by God series – bringing healing and wholeness to your heart and soul

Broken Dreams, Mended Heart

Broken Dreams, Mended Family

Broken Dreams, Mended Marriage

I Do – Again: a devotional for remarrieds

Second Chances and Second Cups: A short story collection.

The Physics of Love

The Mystery of Christmas Inn, Colorado

Christmas Under the Stars

Transformation – a devotional

The Oregon Trail Mysteries series

Kate

A Pink Lady Thanksgiving

Hearts of the Pony Express series

Hollenberg Hearts

Written in Love series

Cactus Lil and the City Slicker

Mail-Order Romance series

New Hope Train

Books by Donna Schlachter

Available at Online Retailers and Fine Booksellers:

Quiet Moments Alone with God: a devotional

100 Answers to 100 Questions About Loving Your Husband

Double Jeopardy: a novel about murder, mining, and a mock marriage

Detours of the Heart – MISSadventure Brides Romance Collection

"Ye shall know the truth, and the truth shall make you free."

John 8:32

First and foremost, to God, the Father; Jesus, the Son,

And the Holy Spirit. Without them, no story would be worth telling

To my husband, Patrick. My biggest fan and supporter.

French Icarian Colony, Iowa

October 1868

Chapter 1

Doctor Julia Brown—no, alias Julia Belvedere now—leaned her head against the scratchy horsehair seat of the stagecoach as it rounded a bend into the last stop on her ticket—Quincy, Iowa. Sweat plastered her hair to the nape of her neck, and dust coated everything, including her seven traveling companions.

Not truly companions, of course. With a secret as looming as the one she shoved into the pit of her stomach, anybody she met from this point on could be nothing more than an acquaintance.

Squished between two men on the only forward-facing seat, she drew a breath through clamped teeth as the driver careened around yet another corner. The weight of the men compressed her ribs and shoulders, and she'd quickly learned to prepare for the onslaught of discomfort in advance.

The man on her right—a banker, he said—nodded to her, a lopsided grin lifting the left corner of his mouth. "Ma'am."

The oaf on her left grunted and leaned toward the window, granting her an extra couple of inches of space. She'd endured four days of his stench of unwashed body and clothes perfumed with cheap rotgut whiskey. When he boarded at the first stop west of Des Moines, the smell gagged her. She sniffed in his general direction. He seemed no riper than yesterday. Had the odors assaulted her olfactory receptors to the point of dulling them? Or did she not notice the difference because now all the passengers smelled the same? She certainly hoped the former.

Julia took advantage of the space to pull a much-used and almost-unrecognizable handkerchief from her reticule. Dabbing at the perspiration on her forehead and cheeks, she sighed at the sight of the now-gray cotton. Dusty, like the rest of her clothes. Her skin. Her world. And her future.

The driver, a scrawny man with a mustache almost to his chest, banged on the roof of the coach. "Quincy coming up."

Julia peeked past the banker for a glimpse of her new home. At least for the meantime. Until she could earn enough to purchase another ticket to somewhere else. Where that was, she had no idea. Depended on how much and how soon. She sighed. Quincy looked like a stop on the trail, not much more. A main street through, a dozen or so businesses including two saloons and a mercantile, and half a dozen houses were all she could spy from this angle.

When the stagecoach lurched to a stop, she rued the lack of pressure from her seatmates. While creating an intimately uncomfortable and hot environment, she now wished they'd stayed as they were. Before she could plant her feet out in front of her, she slid from the bench onto the floor and onto her derriere.

Thankfully, her skirts remained in place, so only the tops of her button-up boots and the frilly hem of her petticoat showed, but still—most unbecoming.

Six sets of hands reached for her—the oaf couldn't bother to help, he laughed so hard—and she finally accepted the banker's offer. While they'd not exchanged more than a dozen words,

11

having sat in close proximity for the past days—well, the others were strangers, weren't they?

The door popped open, and the driver stuck his head in. "Ever'body off who's gettin' off."

She clambered to her feet, straightened her skirts, and pressed her shoulders back. Her cheeks burned, but she would not permit this experience to disarm her. She nodded to the banker. "Thank you, sir." A glance at her other bench mate silenced him. "At least some are gentlemen in this area."

The finance man released her hand and tipped his hat. "Ma'am."

The driver offered his arm, and she stepped out of the coach and into the late afternoon sunlight. She paused, blinking until her eyes adjusted. Her first impressions were correct.

Quincy proved itself little more than a watering hole in the desert.

She exhaled and gathered her skirts in one hand, side-stepping a road apple directly in front of her. "My carpetbag, please."

With little time to pack and not knowing exactly how and where she'd travel, she'd limited her items to a single small bag, one she could carry herself if necessary. From the looks of this town and the stage stop, nobody expected a porter. The driver called to a young boy astride the luggage on top of the coach. The boy dug under several packages and cases, then dropped her bag over the side and onto the ground.

She grimaced, praying her grandmother's mirror and her mother's crystal perfume atomizer weren't damaged. And if they were? Another exhale. She'd live without them. Because no matter how many mementoes of the past, little mattered from here on out. Her vocation, her very name, wrenched from her through no fault of her own.

Despite what the coroner in Des Moines said.

She gripped her bag in her free hand and crossed the street to the nearest hotel. A hot bath, a decent meal, and a soft bed would restore her faith that this desperate plan she'd come up with had merits. She stepped inside, hope rising like bubbles in that fine bath.

A few minutes later, she exited and paused on the boardwalk, clutching a slip of paper in the fingers that also lifted her skirts from the dirt and squalor of the town.

With only two dollars to her name and no job in sight, she couldn't afford even the smallest of rooms in the dingy establishment. According to the clerk, Mrs. Murphy had an

13

opening.

And although she brought the hotel no business, the clerk proved gracious enough to allow her a few minutes to freshen up in a small powder room, including a liberal dose of rosewater to disguise the odors of her travel at least partially.

Julia passed a saloon, the swinging doors doing little to disguise the goings-on inside. Fancy women sashayed around the tables, feathers decorating their hair and their scantily clad forms. Men played cards or drank, and smoke thickened the air. Keeping her eyes focused on the walk ahead, she promised herself she'd never get to where she had to consider working in a place like that.

Following the directions given by the clerk at the hotel, she made two turns off the main road before slowing in front of a two-story house. The street faded off into the surrounding the windswept grassland as if it had forgotten its direction or intention.

Much like the houses and probably its occupants. She studied the surrounding houses. Faded paint. Faded flowers. A faded woman sitting on a front porch shelling peas or beans.

The residence she sought bore a SHARED ROOM FOR RENT sign in a window. Honestly, she'd hoped for her own space, private, a sanctuary of sorts. Still, beggars couldn't be choosers. Hopefully, the sign contained current information, although the placard looked old as the hills.

She switched her carpetbag to her other hand and pushed in through the gate. Her footsteps crunched on the gravel walkway, but the steps and front stoop looked solid enough and didn't sag beneath her.

She knocked on the door and waited just a moment before a woman as old as Methuselah's mother opened it.

Bright blue eyes peered out from behind gold-rimmed spectacles, much like the pair Julia carried in her reticule. "Yes?"

"The man at the hotel suggested I contact you. I need lodging."

"Come in."

Julia stepped into a darkened hallway. Burgundy and green striped wallpaper lent a classic tone to the foyer, and an oak staircase shot up through the middle of the space. Several doors opened off the hallway leading to the kitchen, she supposed, as delectable smells of meat, vegetables, and fresh bread wafted toward her.

The wizened elf-lady, who stood below her shoulder, offered her hand. "I'm Mrs. Murphy. I own the place."

"What is the price, please?"

"Shared is five bits a week."

"Does that include any meals?"

"Breakfast and supper. Midday will be on your own." The landlady leaned closer. "Although there's usually enough left from the night before to make yourself a sandwich."

"Who might I share with?"

"Well, it might be with me." Mrs. Murphy cackled. "Then again, maybe not." She patted Julia's forearm. "A girl from the saloon. She isn't a fancy woman. Don't cotton to that sort here. Cleans, does laundry, looks after those soiled doves. They pay her real good."

"I'll also need to seek employment. What sort of wage might I expect to earn?"

"Well, she makes about two dollars a week, mostly from tips. I think her wages is about a dollar."

"Do you know of other employment?"

Mrs. Murphy chuckled as she sized her potential boarder up and down. "Well, now, don't you talk real fancy? I hear John Bacon at the mercantile needs a girl for behind the counter. You're a little older, so he might take you on for six bits a week, maybe a little more if you work hard."

16

Six bits? With the room costing five a week, that left only one to put aside. A ticket from here to as far as she could go—California—would surely cost in the range of one hundred dollars. Eight hundred bits. Almost a thousand weeks of saving. And if she ever got sick, or needed new shoes, or—what was she thinking? She couldn't stay here for twenty years.

Which left the saloon. The very place she'd sworn never to darken the threshold of. A quick calculation rendered the horrible truth of her situation. To earn enough to leave this town within a year, she needed employment that netted her more than fifteen bits per week.

She would have to shorten her next trip or lower her standards drastically.

"If I don't eat breakfast, could you lower the price?"

"You staying here will raise the atmosphere of my place. How's about the shared room, four bits including two meals? You choose which two."

Her knees wobbled at the woman's generosity. She offered her hand, which Mrs. Murphy promptly shook. "You have a deal."

"Come on, I'll show you the room. Molly is clean and quiet, and I think you two will get along grand."

17

Getting along with a roommate was the last thing on Julia's mind right now.

Getting out of this town and as far away as possible from Des Moines was the prime goal.

~ ~ ~

Josiah Klemp grunted under the weight of the basket of produce. It weighed less than a Thanksgiving turkey, yet it felt more like an elephant. He gritted his teeth, sweat trickling down his spine as he neared Mrs. Murphy's boardinghouse. The old lady, one of his best customers, always got the pick of his offerings.

He set the delivery on the front stoop and knocked. As he waited, he glanced around. The ROOM FOR RENT sign didn't show in the front window any longer. He noticed things like that. Not that folks appreciated his attention to detail. At least, not in Quincy.

He straightened and shrugged the kinks and aches from his back, pausing at the sharp twinge under his shoulder blades. He needed a more sedentary job. Hadn't the field doctor warned him against too much movement? The pieces of metal still embedded in his body could move. Might slice a vein. Or an— what did the man call it? An ar-ter-ee? Like a vein, but different.

18

Well, here he stood, three years after his army service, and still no stronger physically than a babe. He a grown man, with a daughter to care for and raise, barely able to lift his boots unless he wore them.

Footsteps tripped down the stairs and headed in his direction. Likely a boarder, sent by the landlady to answer his summons. Which one would it be today? Molly? No, probably working. Perhaps Mr. Gerard, the schoolteacher? Nah, he should be with his students.

The door opened, and he took a step back. A vision of loveliness stood before him. Smiling at him. Not beautiful as most men would deem, but indeed comely. Her curly hair, the color of the leaves on the oak tree at the corner of the house— sun-kissed, golden yet orange at the same time—framed her face and flowed over her shoulders like molten lava.

She glanced at the vegetables at his feet. "Hello. Mrs. Murphy thought she recognized your knock."

How to answer that? His tongue stuck to the roof of his mouth as he stood there, dumbstruck. Was this the new lodger?

She held out a hand toward him, and he itched to smother it between his own. Instead, he jammed his fists into his pockets, ashamed of the callouses and rough skin. "Shall I take the basket?"

Of course, she didn't know the way Mrs. Murphy operated. He swallowed hard, praying for saliva to loosen his tongue. "No, I'll carry it. To the kitchen." To prove his words, he hefted the basket, biting back a grunt. He'd never show himself weak to a woman so sensitive as she. "I know the way."

She stepped back and gestured him inside. As he passed her in the hallway, the delicate scent of rosewater tickled his nose. Her light footsteps behind him reminded him of his daughter. But this woman was no child. He wouldn't even call her young. Yet the life shining from her chocolate-colored eyes shouted eternal youth.

He shook his head at his foolish thoughts. Judging by her voice and demeanor, she stood miles out of his class. No doubt passing through town on her way to someplace else, with important plans and an exciting future ahead of her.

Unlike him. Stuck in a small town, in a boy's job, with a daughter to raise. And to hide.

At the end of the hallway, he entered the large kitchen and plopped the wicker basket on the worktable in the center of the room. "Mrs. Murphy usually takes everything I bring."

She stood a few feet away, just out of reach, staring at the floor. "I'm sure it's all fine."

"She usually pays me now, too."

The woman's cheeks colored. "Oh, she didn't mention that." She glanced around the kitchen as though hoping the few coins would magically appear. "I don't know…"

"It's all right. I can come back later."

Please say I can come back later. For one more glimpse of—

He shook himself harder this time. He had no right looking at this woman with longing.

He already had a wife.

Chapter 2

Julia smothered a grin. The poor man's face screamed one emotion after another. A small display of youthful besotting—she got that occasionally, usually from older patients. A dash of internal struggle, as evidenced by the clenched jaws. Then a stiffening of the shoulders—a decision made? A coloring of the cheeks—did she stare at him too much? A deep exhale—or was that a sigh?

Time to ease his plight.

She held out her right hand. "I'm Julia Br—Belvedere. I'm Mrs. Murphy's newest lodger. She is retrieving an extra quilt for me, so she asked me to let you in."

"Josiah Klemp."

Julia shook the hand he aimed toward hers, appreciating the firmness. Few things she hated more than cold, clammy, weak handshakes. Like grasping a fish. "I'll ask her about the bill."

Not allowing him to respond, she dashed up the stairs, feeling like a child again. Why did this man invoke these feelings in her? Or could her new beginning claim the credit?

Mrs. Murphy turned from the bed in her shared room. "What is it, child?"

"The vegetable man said you usually pay him on delivery."

"Offer him a cup of coffee, and I'll be right down. Don't move as quick as I used to."

Julia skipped down the stairs, along the hallway, and into the kitchen. Apparently, the basket returned with the man, since the selection of potatoes, carrots, rutabagas, parsnips, and half a dozen late-year apples now sat on the table.

She stopped to admire them. "Well, those look really nice. Do you grow them yourself?"

"No. I deliver for Mr. Bacon of the mercantile. Locals grew them, though." He nudged an apple. "I suspect she'll have apple pie or fritters on the menu."

"Mrs. Murphy said to offer you coffee. The way she talks,

24

she might not make it downstairs until the cows come home."

He chuckled, a pleasing rumble like the purring of a house cat. She made a mental note to come up with clever statements to elicit a similar response. "That sounds good."

Julia poured them each a cup from the oversized coffeepot simmering on the back of the stove. "Do you take milk or sugar?"

"No, thanks." He sat and waited until she followed suit, then sipped. "I believe she has the best Java in town."

"Do you enjoy working at the mercantile?"

He shrugged, and a tiny grimace flitted across his face. Was he in pain? Should she ask? No, best to keep quiet. No point letting folks know of her interest in anything medical. Still, she would keep watch. Perhaps she could suggest a liniment to ease his discomfort.

"Family?"

"A daughter."

She pondered their conversation. Was she being too forward? Perhaps Quincy was more constrained than Des Moines. Which could be good for her. Made keeping her secret easier.

So what secrets did Mr. Kemp strive to keep? Perhaps she'd

put him at ease by offering information about herself. Not the truth, of course. Far too dangerous. Just enough for him to think of her as simply an ordinary person.

She set her cup down. "No family for me. I'm an only child. Parents dead." All true so far. "Passing through town." Truth, again. Even if circumstances indicated she'd be here a while. "Looking for honest work."

He stared at her, then his eyes narrowed. "What can you do?"

"Read and write. Do math. I'm strong."

She caught his wince at that declaration. Did he think she mocked his lack of flexion and strength? She hurried to explain. "For a woman, of course."

His shoulders relaxed, and he leaned back in his chair. "I knew what you meant."

She waited. He had more to say, but she couldn't rush him. Of this, she was certain.

"Mr. Bacon is looking for help."

She sighed. "Mrs. Murphy mentioned that job to me. Behind the counter."

"Yes, but he also needs somebody who has the skills you do, too. He's kind of rusty, he says, with his numbers. I suspect he never went beyond the third grade or so."

Julia leaned forward. "Do you know how much it pays?"

"Heard him say he'd pay up to two dollars a week. Said he's putting an ad in the classifieds in the Des Moines paper, he's so desperate to find help."

"Sounds perfect. Thank you."

But instead of looking pleased, he grunted, downed his coffee, and stood. "Gotta go."

Mrs. Murphy's footsteps sounded along the hallway. "Hold your horses. I'm'a comin'. Got'cher money right here." She dropped several coins into his hand then saw him to the door. "I'll take apples any time you have 'em."

"Yes, ma'am."

He tipped his hat to Julia's landlady, then exited the house, leaving a vacuum the size of Texas where he once sat.

Why had his face melted at her interest in the position? If he didn't want her working at the same business, why mention it at all?

This man—and his secret—ran deep as the Mississippi.

~ ~ ~

Stupid. Stupid. Stupid.

Josiah trudged toward the mercantile to pick up his next

27

delivery, berating himself for mentioning the same job he sought. He, too, could read and write. And do sums. Some. Probably not as well as Miss Julia.

Then again, she would likely excel at any task she undertook.

He'd known her but a few minutes and already saw deep into her soul. She had secrets, too, which so far, she hadn't shared with him. And why should she? He hadn't told her the exact truth, had he?

And now he'd gone and blabbed about the very job he wanted. The one he needed to support his daughter and himself. The position that would pay enough so he could save for their trip west. Away from Marie's mother.

His wife.

Oh, yes. No matter the fact he hadn't seen her since taking his daughter two years ago and running this far on the few dollars he'd scraped together. No matter he'd tried long and hard to forget what she'd done to Marie.

None of that made any difference. He needed to make more money. His little girl went to sleep many nights with a near-empty belly, and he'd taken in several notches on the leather strap holding up his britches.

Stupid, yes, but no fool. An employer, presented with Miss Julia, a woman of breeding and gentility and education, or himself, mostly self-taught and very rough around the edges, he knew who *he'd* hire.

So why had he opened his big mouth and blabbed about the best job currently available in town? Showing off? Letting her know he knew something she didn't?

Or perhaps because he sincerely wanted to help her?

He slowed to a halt at a corner. "Lord, help me be the man You want me to be. To be a father to Marie. And a friend to Miss Julia. She sure looks like she could use one."

A weight the size of the Rock of Gibraltar lifted from his shoulders, and he continued his way to the mercantile and Mr. Bacon.

First thing, he'd tell his boss about the new lady's interest in this plum position.

Then he'd check the trash bins behind the shop for unsellable but not-quite-rotten fruit and vegetables for their supper tonight. Maybe he'd tell Marie the Stone Soup story again. To disguise his inability to provide properly for her.

Again.

Chapter 3

Julia shrugged back her shoulders and lifted her chin. Yes, she needed work. But that didn't mean she must beg for it. No, she'd go in, talk to Mr. Bacon. Disclose her more-than-adequate skills. Surely, he'd see her education, reliability, and personable manner.

Hopefully, he wouldn't see past her thin veneer of respectability to the haunting shadows in her soul surrounding the death of the child. Which was *not* her fault. Had his parents brought him in sooner, she could have operated before the appendix ruptured. Instead, she'd spent six futile hours cleaning the boy's abdominal cavity of the mass of infection.

To no avail. Henry Morgan, three days shy of his seventh birthday, now lay cold in his grave.

That hadn't stopped the furor of the parents, however. Nor the allegations that—because she was a woman—her medical training was less credible than a man's would be. Naysayers said women didn't have scientific minds capable of absorbing the thousands of details about the human body that a man could. Sure, female doctors could tend to women with child, but not to men with a broken leg. Or children with serious internal maladies. Despite their nurturing nature.

She swallowed back the words battling for release at the unfairness of the judgment of the parents—and others—who knew nothing of medical practice. But what of the condemnation of her male peers? And the rubber-stamping of the man elected as coroner? The one whose only medical experience rose to the level of knowing how to stop a nosebleed.

She exhaled. Someday, coroners might actually be trained as a medical doctor. And someday, an examination of a body could prove cause of death scientifically, not merely from assumptions, half-truths, and outright lies. And grieving parents' accusations.

She paused as she pushed through the door into the mercantile, allowing her eyes to adjust from the brightness of the early morning. Today, she wasn't applying as a doctor. Today, she was simply a woman from Des Moines—no, better make that Pittsburgh. Surely nobody in this small town ever traveled that far. Surely, she'd not have to answer questions for which she had no answers.

A portly man with more hair on his chin than his head beamed across the counter at her. "Welcome to our little establishment, Miss."

Julia stifled a smile. At her age, most assumed her matrimonial status earned her a *ma'am*. Well past thirty and racing toward forty, she appreciated his kindness nonetheless. "Thank you. Mr. Bacon?"

He blinked twice, then nodded. "How can I help you?"

She stepped forward and offered her hand. "I'm here to help you." When he gently but firmly returned the gesture, she smiled. "I understand you are looking for somebody to help with accounts and such."

"Where did you hear that?"

"Mr. Klemp." Her heart thudded in her shoes. Was she here on a fool's errand? "Perhaps you've already filled the position?"

"Mr. Klemp?" His brow pulled down a moment, then he nodded again. "Josiah. He told you about the position?"

"Yes." She shifted from one foot to the other. "Did I misunderstand?"

"No. Not at all. I just thought he wanted that job for himself." He chuckled. "There I go, jumping to conclusions. The wife says it's the only exercise I get."

Mr. Klemp desired this job? Then why would he tell her about it? Had he thought she wouldn't apply? Or that Mr. Bacon preferred a man? She resisted stomping a booted foot. Why did men control every aspect of business, finance, medicine, and education? Not because a woman couldn't. No, they seemed to work diligently to keep women in the home, raising children. Quiet and out of the public eye.

Well, this was 1868, for goodness' sake. Not 1768.

She drew a deep breath. "Is the position still available?"

"Um, yes, it is. You can read and write? Do math?"

She gritted her teeth. Not only had she graduated from normal school, but she'd also attended medical school. She could do long division in her head. Fractions of milligrams needed in medicines formed her everyday thought life. Yes, she could do math. And biology. And chemistry. And anatomy.

But she couldn't—wouldn't speak of these matters. Instead, she smiled and pushed away the lump in her throat. "Why don't you test me?"

"Test you?" Sweat dotted his prominent forehead. "How?"

"Give me an invoice from a supplier. I will calculate the cost of each item, add on your profit, and suggest your retail price."

"You can do all that?"

How had the man run his business up to this point if he couldn't even manage those simple calculations? "Yes. Where is your workroom?"

He lifted the counter access door and stepped back to allow her to precede him. "In through that curtain. The desk."

Julia nodded and followed his directions, smiling when he trailed along behind her. As she stepped through the cloth barrier, she groaned. A pile of papers the size of a wheelbarrow huddled against the far wall. She gasped silently. At least, she hoped he hadn't heard. It appeared Mr. Bacon hadn't addressed his accounts in some time.

She paused and faced him. "Is this what I think it is?"

He dropped his chin to his chest and nodded.

"How have you managed?"

He shrugged. "I pay the amount at the bottom of the page."

She exhaled then pulled out the cane-back chair, also drowning in a ream of papers. After placing that stack on the floor, she perched on the seat and picked up a sheet from the top of the pile. A nub of a pencil in the top drawer would suffice. She retrieved her spectacles from her reticule and slipped them on, adjusting them for focus. "Let's see. You received twenty-four cans of sweetened condensed milk." She jotted the price for the case on the reverse of the invoice, divided to find the cost per can. "Okay. How much do you mark up your inventory?"

"Mark up?"

"Yes, the difference between what you pay and what you receive. To pay overhead, salaries, and a little for yourself."

Mr. Bacon huffed out his chest. "Depends on what it is. Things that keep, like canned goods, a little less because there's no spoilage. Meat, eggs, fresh milk, produce, a little more."

"Sweetened condensed milk?"

"Two cents more a can."

"That's less than ten percent. That seems low."

His brow lowered, eyebrows meeting in the middle. "You telling me how to run my business?"

"Mr. Bacon, are you the only mercantile in town?"

"Yes. Why?"

"Folks aren't likely to travel into the next town to purchase what they need, are they?"

"Not unless they're already going there for something else."

"Does that happen often?"

"No."

She set the pencil on the desk. "Then I think you could increase your mark up a little, don't you?"

"But that's the same price since I opened the mercantile. Don't want folks to think I'm stealing from them."

"How long have you been in business?"

"More'n thirty years."

"Have you increased prices at all during that time?"

"Not unless the supplier does. Take those cans, for example. Used to pay eight cents for them. Charged ten. Now they're a whole dime. I charge twelve cents."

"The same profit even though the price increased? That's just not good business sense, Mr. Bacon. You aren't stealing from your customers. They're stealing from you."

"What would you charge?"

"Fourteen cents. That's four cents per can to cover expenses. When you sell the entire case, that's less than a dollar profit." She leaned toward him. "How long does it take you to sell all twenty-four cans?"

"I get a new case every three months. Except in November and December. Then I get a case each month on account of the holidays and extra baking."

"What do you say? Should we be bold?"

"If I lose business—"

"I don't believe you will. If you do, we'll drop the price again." She returned to the invoice. "Now, let's talk about these other items, shall we?" She peered at him over her spectacles. "Assuming I have the job?"

A slow nod from Mr. Bacon settled the butterflies in her stomach, and she sealed their verbal agreement with a slow smile.

One hurdle overcome. With a job under her belt, she could settle in, save her money, and plan her next move.

With any luck, she'd be on her way by Christmas.

A new life in the New Year. Had a nice ring to it.

~ ~ ~

Josiah stepped down from the covered wagon parked behind the mercantile, rubbing his arms to ward off the early morning chill. Behind him, Marie stirred beneath a mountain of quilts and horse blankets.

He patted the wagon tail. "Stay abed, child. I'll get a fire started and see about finding us something to eat."

"Okay, Papa." His daughter's blue eyes, a reflection of his own, peeked above the covers. "I'm hungry."

"Me, too."

Indeed, his stomach growled and grumbled, complaining his throat had been cut. What little food he had fed his daughter, with him pretending to eat the same six beans over and over as she gobbled down the rest. A couple of handfuls of dried beans didn't go far. Not with a growing and active child to feed, besides an adult. Not that he'd consider himself active. Or at least, not as active as he'd like.

After gathering kindling and a few sticks from under the wagon, he used his army flint to catch the flame. Cupping the tiny ember between his hands, he blew softly, breathing life into it. Sitting back on his haunches, he pondered the sermon on Sunday, about how God breathed into man. What a miracle—simply the act of inhaling and exhaling. Necessary to every living creature. And that humankind served as the only recipient of the Almighty's respiration.

He held his hands to the flames, warming them before

standing. "Fire's on, Marie. I'll be back in a few minutes."

He headed along the alley toward the bakery a few doors down, past the tailor shop and the closed doctor's office. Not that he had much call for either—no money for frivolities such as a new suit or medical care. Thankfully, the mercantile carried ready-made dungarees and shirts for him, as well as simple shifts and underthings for Marie. Another expense he could ill-afford—the child grew out of her clothing every year. As for a doctor—well, even if he needed one and could afford to pay for the service, Quincy hadn't attracted a new medico since Doc Whipple died a year ago.

Sure enough, on the trash bin outside the bakery door, a paper-wrapped parcel charitably provided by Abigail, the spinster woman in her late forties who ran the shop. Who'd also set her cap for him when he first landed in town. Who he lied to and said his wife planned to join him shortly.

She'd taken the news graciously, but he suspected her generosity in providing yesterday's pastries grew from her concern for his daughter more than for him. After all, what self-respecting husband would appear in town with a child and no wife? And what respectable woman wouldn't join her husband in two years? No, she saw through his subterfuge, yet kept her own counsel regarding the truth.

Josiah snatched the package, turned on his heel, and headed back to his daughter. A sour taste rose in the back of his throat as he considered his sorry predicament. How he thought he could raise a child on his own escaped him. He could barely look after himself. Yet he couldn't leave her with that vile and cruel woman who birthed her.

Arriving at the wagon, he raised the food in the air. "Breakfast is served, milady."

Marie emerged from the wagon, clambering down like an escaped monkey. "Papa, what did you bring us today?" She rubbed her hands together. "Homemade bread? Maybe with butter? And jam?"

Unlikely Abigail would include the toppings, but then again, he never knew. Somehow, the woman remembered Marie's birthday each year and provided a small cake he was certain she'd baked fresh for the child.

He sat on the stump and beckoned his daughter to settle on her makeshift stool. Fingers shaking from the cold, or from hunger, or perhaps from anticipation, he fumbled with the string and paper, both of which he tucked into his pocket for use later. Marie wriggled and leaned across the small fire, eyebrows high and smile wide.

He opened the inner parchment paper and held it for her inspection. "Jam tarts. A slice of peach pie. And—" He inhaled deeply. "Lemon squares."

"Oh, Papa, my favorite!" Her smile faltered. "But I'll share with you."

He tore the paper and handed her favorite to her. "No. I'll enjoy the pie. And there are two tarts, one for each of us."

Wishing for coffee for himself and milk for his daughter, but making do with water from his canteen, he practically inhaled the food. Not a lot to fuel either of them for the day, but enough to hold body and soul together.

At least until supper.

He glanced at their home on wheels. Perhaps he should load them up and head out of town in search of better-paying work for him. Miss Belvedere likely had the position at the mercantile. The one he desperately needed to sustain his hopes of succeeding in his new role as single support for his daughter. And his hopes of being more than a cripple.

Or he could sell the wagon and team of horses. Paying to keep the two beasts at the livery by working two hours every evening seemed a waste of time and energy. Neither of which he had in excess. Why, he could likely fetch at least fifty or sixty dollars for all. They could live on that for a year, along with what he earned.

He popped the final pastry into his mouth, chewed, and swallowed. Then he grinned at his daughter. "What would you think about living in a proper house again?"

"We're not going back to Pittsburgh, are we, Papa?" Marie's mouth turned down. "You said we wouldn't ever go back there."

"No. Maybe we'll go somewhere that doesn't have snow. How does that sound?"

"Like a dream."

Hopefully a sweet one, and not a nightmare.

Chapter 4

Julia pushed back from the desk and stretched her arms high in the air. She glanced at the Regulator clock on the wall of the workroom.

Four hours hunched over paperwork had garnered her cramped muscles, tired eyes, and four stacks of paperwork. All evidence of progress.

Her stomach growled, reminding her the noon hour had come and gone. In her excitement of meeting Mr. Bacon and perhaps getting gainful employment, she'd eaten little breakfast and neglected to prepare food for her midday meal. He thoughtfully brought coffee earlier, alleviating her thirst.

Voices filtered from the store into her hearing, and she crossed the small area to listen. Through the space between the curtains, she spied two women chatting while selecting potatoes from a bin at the rear of the store.

The older one tsk-tsked as she discarded one after the other. "I don't know what those people at that commune are thinking. Maybe they believe we don't know the difference between a good potato and a bad one."

"Usually, their produce is so good." The other woman, a few years younger and with a toddler in tow, nodded. "What do you think they do out there?"

"Up to no good, I suspect. The reverend says they are communists. They share everything."

"Well, Violet, he also said that the early church sold all and shared with those in need."

Apparently, this Violet woman didn't need—or want—reminding. "Perhaps so. But *they* were Christians. I've heard these people don't believe in God." She leaned closer. "I've also heard that children go missing once they move in."

"Missing? Do you mean—"

Violet sniffed and waved a hand as if to dismiss the

woman's concerns. "Just telling you what I heard. Not that I'm one to pass on gossip, mind you."

The younger woman's cheeks sported spots of pink. "Of course not."

Julia chuckled softly. Violet's sidekick proved wise beyond her years by choosing not to confront the woman on her flagrant rumor-mongering.

The older woman moved on, still holding one potato. "Although why anybody would steal children is beyond my comprehension."

As are most things, no doubt.

The toddler tugged on her mother's hand. "Mama, may I have a sweet, please?"

Her mother patted the child's cheek. "I cannot imagine the pain of losing one of my own. No matter how many I might have."

"Well, if you want to keep them, don't let them out of sight."

"Have any gone missing any since these people built their colony outside town?"

"Not yet."

"They seem so nice. I can't imagine—"

"Heathens, I suspect."

"Really?"

"Do you ever see them in church?"

"No, but I heard they sometimes have hymn sings or Bible reading on Sunday evenings."

"They aren't like the Amish and the Quakers. The Old Orders live separate lives with plenty of strange rules, but they believe. And just because somebody plants themselves in a pew doesn't mean they belong there. For some folks, it's a way to fit in."

While I'm no expert in how a real Christian lives, sounds like she's talking about herself.

"Why would somebody want to live like that, I wonder?"

Violet sniffed. "Perhaps they are pagans."

Mr. Bacon crossed the mercantile in her view. "Greetings, ladies. Anything I can help with?"

The older woman held up the potato. "Just look at that. Misshapen. How do we know it's fit to eat?"

"Everything I sell is fit to eat, as you put it. Or I'll replace it for you."

The younger woman pursed her lips. "I don't know. Can we really trust people who don't fear the Lord not to poison us?"

The proprietor chuckled. "If you're talking about the folks at the Icarian Commune, many believe in God, so far as I know."

"Why aren't they in church?"

"It's a long ride from there to here. More'n nine miles. Half a day just one way."

"No excuse."

He removed, then cleaned his spectacles with the edge of his apron. "They seem neighborly. Invite the town to their socials. Come here to ours. And I've talked to several when they come in with hams and such." He quirked his chin toward the potato in Violet's hand. "That wasn't one of theirs, by the way. Seth Holden grew it in his field near the Nodaway River."

"As I said, doesn't mean anything." Violet looked down her nose at the man. "What else do you know about them?"

"They share all the work. They own the property in common. They do their job and mind their own business. Eggs are always fresh, and their bread—" He closed his eyes and rubbed his ample stomach. "What else is there to know?"

Julia covered her mouth with a hand. If these three knew she eavesdropped, she might not learn any more. In fact, this Icarian place sounded perfect. While she'd remain on her guard

49

and not reveal her medical training, surely they'd find her suitable work. An answer to prayer.

If she prayed.

But his explanation hadn't appeased the older woman. "If it's so perfect, why don't more people join?"

"Not everybody holds their earthly possessions so loosely as to surrender them at the door. Plus, there's the admission fee."

Julia leaned closer.

Admission fee?

Violet sniffed. "Knew there was something. Imagine charging folks money to work for free."

"Yep, they pay sixty dollars to cover the costs to run the place, and to ensure they don't attract just indigent and lazy folks looking for a handout."

Violet gasped. "Sixty dollars. Why, you could buy a house for that." She dropped the potato into the bin. "I just remembered. I have enough of these for now." She nudged her friend. "Come along. I want to stop at the bakery on the way home. I need some *real* bread."

After the two left the shop amidst a flood of rustling skirts and confidential titters, Julia returned to her task. While the commune sounded like a solution to her dilemma, perhaps not.

She had no money to enter a community where she'd work out the rest of her natural days for free. She needed to put more distance between her and Des Moines. And the past. Without money, she couldn't move on.

Mr. Bacon poked his head into the room. "The missus has my dinner on the table. Would you mind watching the shop while I eat? I'll bring you down a plate after."

"That's most kind, but unnecessary. You don't need to feed me as well."

He waggled his fingers at her. "You have more than earned your pay today. Already I've had two customers who commended me on raising the price of the canned sweet milk. They believe it must be better than the brand I carried before."

"Very well. Instructions?"

"You already have what you need. A mind. And you can do math. The account book is under the cash box. Extend credit to anybody who asks."

She giggled. "That's something else we may need to discuss."

"Perhaps so, but not on an empty stomach."

She perched on a stool in a corner while he headed upstairs to his wife and his dinner. Judging by the scents wafting down the stairs, meat—perhaps chicken—vegetables, and something apple. Goodness. If she ate midday meal here every day, and breakfast and supper at the boardinghouse, she'd be as big as a barn.

Time passed quickly as she tallied ledgers and adjusted prices, along with serving three customers. Before she knew it, Mr. Bacon returned and set a heaping plate on the desk.

She straightened and set her pen down. "Thank you. And please thank Mrs. Bacon for me."

When she picked up her fork and stabbed at a chunk of potato, he cleared his throat. She froze and glanced his direction. His gaze went from the plate to her fork, then to the ceiling.

Heat rose in her cheeks. He expected her to pray.

Except she had not a clue.

Her throat closed off, threatening to choke her as she set her fork down. Would she lose the job if she didn't meet Mr. Bacon's religious expectations?

And what of the commune? Perhaps they had similar restrictions. That thought hadn't crossed her mind.

Her shoulders sank beneath the weight of her loss—both of Mr. Bacon's respect and her potential solution to the dilemma facing her regarding her future in Icaria. What a fool she'd been to think either would be so easy to achieve.

No, a curse surely lay on her. First the death of the child, then the false allegations in Des Moines, and now her lack of a spiritual conviction.

What she wouldn't give to have all three erased.

~ ~ ~

Josiah trudged back to his daughter and their meager supper. Thankfully, the saloon owner offered him two crusts of bread and a slice of cheese in exchange for two hours of washing dishes and sweeping floors. Every muscle ached from the added work, but they wouldn't go to bed tonight as hungry as otherwise.

As he passed the mercantile, a light from inside alerted him to another's presence. He glanced at the darkening sky. Almost sundown, yet Mr. Bacon labored on? Seemed out of character for the punctilious older man whose life ran to a strict schedule of hours and minutes.

He crossed the street and peered through the front door and into the retail area. No lamp lit the area. He turned the handle and stepped inside. "Hello?"

The curtain separating the customer space from the work

and storage section rustled, and Miss Belvedere's face appeared between the panels of material. "Yes? Who is it?"

"Josiah Klemp, Miss. We met earlier."

She slipped behind the counter. "Goodness. I didn't realize it was so late. I'm afraid the store is closed, but I'm sure Mr. Bacon wouldn't mind if you purchased something."

He shuffled a toe in the sawdust scattered on the floor. "Not here to buy. Saw the light. Thought something might be amiss."

She chuckled, her entire face relaxing. "Nothing except me working far too long on my first day."

A wisp of a woman like her shouldn't be wandering the streets by herself. Even one who seemed so sure of herself. From the top of her strawberry blonde head to her eyes the color of cocoa. Deep pools of thought peering out from behind those gold-rimmed round spectacles. Which she kept pushing back up her nose.

A proper gentleman would offer to walk her home. Not that he was in that class, although he strove for honor and integrity. And a genuine lady like her wouldn't accept such an offer from a man like him. No, siree. She deserved much better.

After they stared at each other, her tongue as seemingly tied into knots as his own, he drew up his shoulders. Even a crippled messenger boy as protector was better than none. "If'n you're heading to the boarding house, I could accompany you." When her cheeks pinkened, he attempted to explain himself. "I mean, so's you're not going alone. Just in case."

She nodded. "Let me grab my hat and reticule. You'd honor me by escorting me home. If it's not out of your way."

Before he had time to explain how his home—behind the livery barn—was directly across the street from her own, she disappeared. Instead, he clamped his mouth shut. The room in the back went dark, and she came out again, all a-flurry with tying on her bonnet and slipping her hand through the drawstrings of her bag.

On the boardwalk, he paused as she closed and locked the door, then held out his arm. "Just so you don't trip in the dark."

She hesitated, then slid her arm into his. Her touch sent a tingle that raced up his arm, jolting his heart until it skipped and skimmed, rattling against his ribs. Seemed its uneven beat kept time with his limp, accentuating and echoing his physical failings for all to hear. Down the steps and across the side street, where he paused again at the gate to Mrs. Murphy's house. His back and leg ached from the effort of walking straight with his shoulders pressed back. He would not embarrass her by having her seen in public with a cripple, despite the late hour.

She dipped her head. "Thank you, Mr. Klemp. Your arrival was most fortuitous."

Was she mocking him? After all, they'd passed but two businesses—one shuttered for the night as the other opened for business with the sunset—and not a single drunk on the street.

Stop looking for offense where she intends none.

He touched the brim of his hat. "You're most welcome."

She glanced at the house, then back to him. "Have you heard of the Icaria-Quincy Commune?"

Strange question for an obviously educated woman, at least in his estimation. "Sure. 'Spect everybody in these parts has."

"What do you know about them?"

He shrugged, sending a painful stab through his shoulder. "Not much. Seem like friendly folk. Hard workers. Mr. Bacon buys a lot of their goods. Heard they share all the profits equally. Give folks a place to live."

"Do you know if they practice a particular brand of religion, like the Amish and Quakers?"

"Don't know. They don't have a church out there, and the ones who might travel to town come but once a month."

Her shoulders sagged as though a vulture perched there. "Oh."

Had he dashed her hopes with a thoughtless comment? He'd rather cut out his tongue. "Could be a rumor, though. They keep to themselves."

"I heard two ladies talking in the mercantile today. They made the community sound poorly, but Mr. Bacon corrected them. Still, I wonder."

"Are you thinking of joining them?"

"It would solve a lot of problems. Only I don't have the admission fee."

"Right. I heard they had such a thing."

What could he possibly do to help? Truth was, right now, he'd cut off his right arm—no, he wouldn't, either. He had Marie to think about. To protect from her abusive mother. And not just protect. To hide. From *that woman* and the law.

Because a single man on his own couldn't possibly provide the kind of life a little girl needed. Not with him working sunup to sundown. Leaving her to herself in the wagon.

Then a thought struck him. Maybe he could solve Miss Belvedere's problems and his own. If they lived at the commune, they'd have a roof over their heads. Three meals a day. Not likely Marie's mother—or the law—would think of looking for them there.

But how could he help all three of them? He'd be lucky to scrape together the admission fee for him and his daughter. He couldn't leave Miss Belvedere.

No, the only way this idea would work was if—no, that was just dumb. He couldn't even suggest—she'd slap his face and walk away. Unless…

… unless he could make her an offer she couldn't turn down. Perhaps she needed a disguise as much as he did. Transform herself into a married woman with a husband and child. Not that their marriage would be real. Or consummated.

Because his wife kept him locked in an unholy matrimony.

Perhaps she, too, could fool whatever—or whoever—she ran from.

Because there was no doubt she fled something. Or somebody.

As much as he needed her, maybe—just maybe—she needed him as much. Or more.

Well, in for a penny, in for a pound.

He drew a deep breath. "I'm just thinking out loud here, but I have a proposition for you."

~ ~ ~

Julia sank onto the bed, careful not to wake Molly. What had she gotten herself into?

In the space of less than two days, she transformed from Doctor Julia Brown, medical doctor, to Julia Belvedere, bookkeeper. And in just five minutes, she listened to a practical stranger suggesting she make yet another change. Although he knew nothing of her past, he offered her the opportunity to become Julia Klemp, wife of Josiah, and mother to Marie.

A child she'd never met.

Of course, a man like Mr. Klemp, so kind and honest, was certain to be married. She'd not thought otherwise.

When she'd asked about his wife, he'd lifted one shoulder, grimaced, and let it drop. "She's no longer with us."

Which was no explanation at all, of course. And he knew it, allowing her to draw her own conclusion. She could be dead. Run off with another man. In an asylum.

Or Josiah could be on the run. Just like her. Two peas in a pod.

What a mess.

She unbuttoned her boots and slipped them off, followed quickly by her stockings, relishing the cool evening air on her bare toes. After relieving herself of her blouse, skirt, various petticoats, and then her corset, she slipped on a cotton shift and lay back on the bed, wishing for the energy to at least wash her face. T'would have to wait. Morning was soon enough.

The punched tin ceiling stared back at her, blurring in the darkness as she relaxed. Josiah's offer included selling his wagon and horse to raise the money for their admission as a family. Her part involved acting the part as his wife, caring for the child. While this solution wouldn't move her further westward, the plan would do.

For now.

But somehow, she must figure out how to raise the money for her ticket out of Quincy. In a few years, once her part of their agreement concluded, when Marie was old enough to take care of her father and his household, she'd leave. Then he could find a real wife. One who would love him and his daughter. Would bear him more children.

What had she gotten herself into?

Chapter 5

Two days later, Josiah headed for the mercantile, Marie's hand in one of his, their few personal items in an old feed sack in the other. He'd hoped to arrive early enough to make a few deliveries, earn his last few coppers. But his leg and back acted up again today, slowing him and hindering his movement. Perhaps he could get some work done later this morning. After—after his wedding. He'd done what he promised—sold the horse and wagon, along with the few meagre sticks of furniture he owned. Marie cried when the preacher loaded their rocking chair in the back of a cart on its way to its new home at the vicarage.

But he had the sixty dollars he needed to buy his way into the Icaria colony. Correction, his, Marie's, and Miss Belvedere's.

In fact, he even had two dollars left over to pay the preacher to wed them.

Today.

Without the wagon to live in, getting married and turning up at the colony must happen immediately.

Up the step from the street, across the boardwalk, he limped. He glanced up at the sky. Dark clouds on the horizon. Perhaps rain loomed. Which could explain his stiffness this early in the day. He pushed his shoulders back, wincing at the sharp pain across his torso. Infirmity in one so young—a mere two years past thirty—didn't bode well. At this rate, completely crippled before he reached forty seemed his certain prognosis.

If he lasted that long.

At least by then, Marie would be out of school, perhaps married with babes of her own. Despite his desire to die in his own bed at a ripe old age, he suspected he'd not receive that wish. Instead, if he could live long enough to see his daughter well-cared for, that would be sufficient.

He set the sack containing his and Marie's belongings on the

62

bench outside the store and pointed to the seat. "Wait here. I'll fetch Miss Belvedere presently." The child sat and folded her hands in her lap. He waggled a finger at her. "Stay here. No running with the boys. Hear me?"

"Yes, Papa."

Inside the mercantile, he paused. Something was different. Somebody organized the shelves in a new way, with the more expensive items at eye level. In the middle of the store, where once the bulk barrels rested, now stood a table. Where flour, sugar, and apples once awaited purchase, now a pair of ladies' gloves, a couple of lace fans, and—what? A woman's hat? Not the typical bonnet that tied under the chin, either. Rather, a delightful piece of pale gray frippery decorated with a satin band and feathers—nestled amidst a length of pink ribbon and a looking glass.

Had Mr. Bacon lost his mind? Surely the women of the town would complain.

"Catches the eye, doesn't it?"

Josiah's head snapped to the proprietor standing beside him. "Sure does."

"Your Miss Belvedere suggested I show the ladies what they can spend their money on besides flour sack britches and

63

baking powder." The older man crossed his arms over his chest. "I had nothing like that in stock, of course. So, she sold me hers. Gave her a whole dollar."

Josiah supposed Miss Belvedere considered she had no use for such items at the Colony. Or perhaps she knew more about the women of this town in three days than he'd learned in all his time here.

Wouldn't surprise him one bit. She was smart. Caught on quick.

Much too much intelligent for the likes of him.

But perhaps Marie could learn much from her. Become more like her. Heaven knew he'd done little in that department. His daughter raced the streets with the boys like one of them. Wild. Uneducated. Yes, he had made the best end of this bargain. Even though their marriage would never consummate, his daughter could become a lady despite her rough beginnings.

The curtain to the work room rustled, and Miss Belvedere stepped through, a half-smile lifting the corners of her lips. Had they always been the color of cherries? How had he not noticed that before? Or did her pale cheeks transfer color to her mouth?

Was she ill? Not slept well? Regretted her decision?

If she reneged on their agreement, what would he do?

Having sold all his earthly belongings, he had nowhere to go. No roof over his daughter's head. Him, he could sleep in a horse trough if necessary. But that would never do for Marie. Entering the colony as a single parent with a daughter did nothing to enhance his disguise. And working for room and board meant he'd never have the resources to leave.

She crossed the store, her smile growing. "Mr. Klemp. Good day." She gestured to the display. "As you can see, I've made good use of my time." She tied her fingers into knots as she twisted the corner of her apron. "And I've told Mr. Bacon I won't be able to work for him every day since you and I are marrying."

Ah, so she'd crossed that bridge. He'd not given much thought to the man or his shop, having little mind for thoughts of anything other than preparing for their move into the Colony.

And their wedding. Which, of course, would come first. Today.

He glanced at the clock on the wall. In less than thirty minutes, in fact.

He held out an arm. "We must hurry as the preacher will think we've changed our minds."

Her smile slipped away, and her brow pulled down. "So soon?"

As usual, he struggled to decipher the meaning behind her words and the tone. Was he rushing her? Had she changed her mind? Her previous words to him about notifying Mr. Bacon she was leaving didn't seem to indicate so. Still...

He nodded. "Yes. In fifteen minutes." He glanced at the proprietor and dipped his head. "I'm sorry that we're both leaving on short notice."

Mr. Bacon chuckled. "I managed for many years on my own. Miss Belvedere worked late these past few days to get my store into fine shape. And she promises to visit and help me with my accounts as often as she can."

Miss Belvedere touched Josiah's forearm. "I spoke with the blacksmith yesterday. He lives at the Colony but works in town every day during the week, depositing his earnings with the Elders on his return each evening to his home and family. Perhaps the leadership would allow us both to work some hours here in addition to at the Colony."

Another chuckle filled the store. "Don't be in such a hurry to get back to work. It's not every day you'll wed." Mr. Bacon peered at each of them, finally fixing his gaze on Miss

Belvedere. "But this does seem a mite rushed. You only came to town a few days ago, and already you're leaving us? Were you not pleased with our arrangement?"

She stepped closer to the older man and gripped his hands. A wave of something akin to jealousy rose in Josiah's chest and threatened to bubble out of his mouth, but he clamped down on the sensation. Why should he mind that Miss Belvedere held the hands of another? There was nothing between them but a business-type relationship.

Surely, nothing like love had blossomed between them, and never would.

Despite the fact she'd saved his life—literally.

~ ~ ~

For Julia, the walk to the church felt more like a funeral procession than her wedding day. What had she done? Grasped at the first solution offered, that's what. She'd not thought through every detail, including how to explain to a little girl that she wasn't her mother and never would be. Or how to fabricate a marital arrangement as flimsy as a cobweb.

And when a misstep or wrong word revealed the subterfuge? Would the Colony be gracious and merciful? Or would the three of them find themselves in a worse situation?

As Marie skipped alongside them, chattering about their new home and how much she missed their horse already, Julia drew several deep breaths to keep her feet moving forward. The girl's braids—not quite parted straight down the back, no doubt the product of her father's ministrations—flip-flopped as she bounced from one foot to the other. A picture of health, her auburn hair streaked with gold from the sun, freckles creating a roadmap across her cheeks and the bridge of her nose, she stood shoulder-high to Julia. When she stood still, that was. Usually she hopped, ran, trotted, or scampered, like a calf let loose in the spring pasture.

Oh, to be that young again.

Prior to her own parents' deaths, she always imagined her father would make this journey with her, to the church and down the aisle, she in a pale gray gown handed down through three generations of women on her mother's side. Her friends and family beaming at her as her papa delivered her to the arm of her groom. Married for life. 'Til death did them part.

But that was before Des Moines. Before a frantic father delivered his seven-year-old son Henry into her hands. Her very capable hands. She still recalled his words of complete trust to her that night.

"Don't know as I cotton to a woman doctoring my boy, but I have no choice. Do your best."

And she had. Except it wasn't enough. The burst appendix had already spread too much infection through the boy's abdomen and into his bloodstream. Nothing she could do. Nothing anybody could have done. Not her. Not a man.

Except Mr. Morgan didn't see it that way. And apparently, he had friends in high places. In the mayor's office. In the newspaper. In the police department. Even in the hospital where she worked. And where his son died.

Within days, she'd lost her position. Another week, her lodgings. The hospital cooperated with the police on a criminal investigation. And Mr. Morgan filed a wrongful death lawsuit with the court.

Suddenly, all her friends disappeared. Nobody received her when she went to their homes and places of business to beg for support to defend her innocence. Acquaintances turned aside in the streets, and boys taunted her with insults and rotten fruit.

Her only choice: leave while she could.

And now here she stood, outside the church, handing over that liberty to a stranger. She knew the law as it regarded marriage. The wife was now under the direction and control of the husband.

Maybe she should take another day to think this out. A week. A month.

She turned to Josiah, but his clenched jaw and down-turned brow suggested she'd best keep her own counsel. Although why this man encumbered himself with a woman who didn't love him, she couldn't understand. Surely there were other women of marriageable age in the town of Quincy who would gladly marry him, care for his daughter as her own, and grant him more offspring?

So why choose her? Did he know her secret? Believe she'd never leave him? Expect that once firmly ensconced in the Colony, she'd have no choice?

Well, she did. She could decide now to leave. She would choose later, for certain. After all, this wasn't a real wedding. Or an actual marriage. Yes, in the eyes of the law, they would now be husband and wife, with all the ramifications of that union. But not to her. They'd agreed. Simply a contract. He'd done his part—provide their admission fee. And she'd do hers—raise his daughter and put up a pretense. For five years, until the girl turned fifteen. Not a day more.

Marie stood on her left and slipped a hand into hers. "Will

you be my new mama now?"

Julia stared down at the child. Sunlight glinted off her hair and lashes almost like a halo. She crouched beside the girl. "Is that what your daddy said?"

Josiah cleared his throat softly, and the girl peered up at him. "He said you needed each other, and you both need me."

Julia straightened and gripped the child's hand. "Did he, now?"

Well, perhaps Josiah told his daughter the truth. Which meant that Josiah Klemp was a deeper river of a man than she'd thought. He also had a secret he needed keeping.

Seemed he suspected she'd kept something from him, too.

Now they were on equal footing.

Ten minutes later, they left the church, Marie tucked into her father's arms, her head lolling on his shoulder. Despite his insistence that he could carry everything, Julia clutched her carpetbag and his feed sack in her hands. Six miles was a long walk with a ten-year-old in his arms, and despite his protests, no doubt painful.

The sun neared the eleven o'clock position, confirmed by the tolling of the church bell as they retraced their steps down Main Street and gained the old Mormon trail road. Thankfully,

71

no heavy rains lately had turned the path into a morass of mud. Still, deep wagon wheel ruts cut through, leaving a narrow shoulder on either side. She followed behind him in single file rather than tread the road opposite him, their strides matching step for step.

About two miles into their journey, the creaking of leather and wood from behind met her ears. She paused and turned. A horse and wagon neared, then slowed.

The driver doffed his hat. "Greetings. Can I give you a ride?"

Josiah set his daughter on her feet, and she grumbled about the rude awakening. "Yes. We are going to the French Icarian Colony. Do you know it?"

"Know it?" He laughed. The horse peered back at him, snorted, and shook its head as though joining in. "I live there. Just coming from Quincy after delivering an order to a man building a house." He waved at the wagon. "I am *Citoyen* Brower, and I run the sawmill. Hop in."

Understanding some French, Julia understood the word pronounced as si-twa-yin to mean citizen, or the communal equivalent of resident. However, Josiah communicated his ignorance of the language with upraised brow. She mouthed the

72

English word to him, and he nodded.

Then Josiah introduced himself and his daughter before stumbling over Julia's name. "This is Miss—Julia. My, um, wife."

He gripped Marie around the waist and hoisted her into the bed of the vehicle while Julia flopped the bags onto the flatbed.

When he turned to her, she shook her head. "I can manage on my own, thank you."

Using the sideboard, she stepped onto the hub of a rear wheel and then flung the other leg over the side, taking care to keep her skirts modestly around her ankles. However, balanced thus, she did not know how to make the last move into the wagon, and stood perched there like a scarecrow in a field, all arms and legs, with no notion of how to control either.

At an unfamiliar touch on her derriere, she shrieked, lost her balance, and tumbled into the wagon, flat on her back, the breath knocked out of her, amidst a flurry of petticoats and skirts.

And laughter.

A few choice words she'd overheard from a very disgruntled Mr. Morgan bubbled to her lips, but without air in her lungs, she couldn't give voice to them. She sat up and pushed her back into position, then frowned at the three faces peering down at her: the driver's, from his perch in the front. Marie's, from where she sat beside her.

And Mr. Klemp's as he knelt over her in the wagon. Looking concerned. Almost. But she'd not worried him as much as she entertained her new husband.

What a way to begin her married life.

Her grandmother's voice echoed in her head: begin as you intend to continue.

While not thrilled at the circumstances she'd landed herself in, she had a choice. She could turn into one of those shrewish women who makes everybody's life an ordeal. Or she could make the best of her situation. At least until she had another option.

She straightened her skirt into place. "Well, now that you've had a demonstration of my tumbling abilities, shall we proceed?"

Marie's eyes widened. "Will you teach me how to tumble, Mama?"

The child's innocent question brought on another round of laughter from the men. The driver, in particular, guffawed from deep in his belly.

Pleased she'd made the better choice, Julia scooted to one side until her back rested against the sideboard. "I may just do that, Marie."

The remaining four miles took less time than the first two, and by the time they arrived at the Colony, Julia's embarrassment had subsided to a sweet memory. Their driver dropped them at the largest building, which he called the Refectory.

He doffed his hat to them. "This is where we eat all our meals. I'll see you at supper, although the cook would probably give you a crust of bread now and deliver you to an elder to settle in."

Julia glanced at the two-story frame building. "So, we don't have our own cooking facilities?"

"No. Communal. Leaves more time for other productive work. You will soon learn."

He chucked the reins, and the wagon pulled away, leaving them standing in a cloud of dust. Julia drew a deep breath, then exhaled, while Josiah picked up their bags. Marie slipped her hand into Julia's and, looking for all the world like a real family, they headed up the walkway to the dining area.

Except Julia knew deep in her heart they weren't a family—

and probably would never be.

Chapter 6

Two hours later, Julia's head ached with the afternoon heat, the stress of the long day, and the interminable droning of the elder assigned to settle them into the community. At least they were now in their own house—such as it was. Not much more than a log cabin with a sod roof. One room. A small pot belly stove centered near the single window beside the door. Despite the chill of the evening, the simple appliance remained as cold as ice. Apparently, permission for fires depended on two things happening: the ice froze in the water pail, and Josiah chopped the wood to fuel the blaze.

With this being their first evening in the community, no wood lay stockpiled in the box inside the door or on the porch. And temperatures, though nearing freezing, hadn't yet occurred.

Perched on the edge of the bed—her cheeks burned when Josiah had sat beside her an hour ago—she silently prayed for Citoyen Marchand to end his lesson. Couldn't he see the child was already asleep on the single bed in the far corner, her cheeks pink with excitement at meeting the other children? How much information did the man really expect them to absorb today?

Perhaps God in His heaven—if He was there at all—finally heard her pleas for help because Cit. Marchand clapped his hands a single time and nodded.

"*Bien*. We will leave it at that for the evening. There is much to learn so that your presence here in Icaria is good for everybody."

Josiah stood. "Thank you. And please thank your dear wife for all the time we've taken from her and your family tonight."

Cit. Marchand waved off the words. "Not a problem. Citoyenne Marchand is accustomed to it." He turned to the door, then paused. "Supper at six. Then a reading in the refectory this evening at seven. We will see you then and you can meet the others. Bring the child, even if she still sleeps."

Julia noted the specific phrasing of his words—attendance was mandatory.

Once the door shut, she collapsed across the bed, her feet still on the floor. Tears burned at the back of her eyes, begging for release. Oh, for a brief respite to cry her heart out. But she would not give in. She hadn't in Des Moines. And she wouldn't here. If she did, she might never surface again.

Instead, she sat up again. She had perhaps an hour to unpack their meagre belongings and make this a little more like a home than a borrowed house. Perhaps Josiah would chop wood—unlikely, given his physical condition. Well, maybe he could unpack, and she could—no, she knew less than nothing about handling an ax. More likely to cut off a toe.

The image of her hopping about on one foot trying to doctor herself brought a smile she didn't know she had. Maybe things weren't as bad as she thought.

Josiah sighed. "Have we made a grave error in coming here?" He glanced at his daughter. "Although she likes the other children she met." He ran his hand through his hair. "So many names to remember."

Julia held up a hand and counted on her fingers. "Louise. Caroline and her brother August." She thought for a moment. "Cit. Marchand's little girl Marie." She paused and tossed him a grin. "Hopefully we won't get the two confused."

"Well, his Marie is but four, so we can at least tell them apart."

He had a sense of humor. Might make the time more bearable. She nodded. "And Henriette and Alexander."

"Don't forget George."

"I did, though, didn't I?"

He chuckled. "I think we both need time. It isn't every day a man—or a woman—weds and moves into a new style of living."

She suspected he'd had his share of unstable living conditions, just as she had. Hopefully, they'd fit in well enough here. For Marie's sake. For Josiah's—funny how easily she went from thinking of him by his formal name and now by his first. Well, they were husband and wife, weren't they?

Yes. And no.

In the eyes of the law.

But what about her?

And what about God?

Because for the first time in her life, as the pastor's words about 'who God joined, let no man tear asunder', echoed in her head, what He thought meant something.

~ ~ ~

After a supper of potatoes, ham, cabbage, then rhubarb cake for dessert, Josiah helped the men rearrange the room for the reading. Of what, he wasn't certain. He'd asked the others sitting at the table he also shared with Miss—Julia and Marie, but they said they didn't know. Apparently, whoever did the reading also did the choosing, both as to content and length. It could be from the Bible, from the writings of Etienne Cabet, the founder of the movement, an article in the French or English newspaper, or something else.

Josiah hoped the piece would at least be in English, although there was no guarantee of that, either.

He glimpsed Miss, um, Julia and his daughter—correction, their daughter—standing along the wall by themselves. After a few minutes, another woman joined them, then another. Judging by their gestures, they introduced themselves to each other. Thankfully, his wife was fluent in French, so communication shouldn't be an issue, although several German, Italian, Russian, and Spanish families also made up the mix of nationalities of the two hundred or so residents.

He grunted as he shoved a stack of chairs toward a burly man who'd introduced himself earlier as Cit. Coubeille, cabinet maker. The man was sound as an ox and built much like one, all neck and shoulders and forearms. Beside him, Josiah felt like a scarecrow. Still, he'd not let his infirmity provide reason to be asked to leave.

Cit. Marchand appeared at his side, giving him a reason to pause, for which he was grateful. "Cit. Klemp, the elders have discussed your situation."

Josiah's heart sank at the somber tone of the man's voice. Too late to prove himself useful, it seemed. Had he said too much earlier regarding his war injuries and limitations? "Can we at least stay tonight so my wife and daughter don't have to travel in the dark?"

"Leave?" Cit. Marchand clapped him on the shoulder. "Not at all. Cit. Bromme needs help in the finer work of harness making and leatherwork. His eyesight is not as good as it was. You will learn under him. Perhaps you will become his apprentice, although you are older than most in that position."

He blinked several times. Sounded like he'd received a promotion from delivery boy to artisan in a single leap. He swallowed hard, trying to shove down the voice whispering in his ear that he would probably mess this up, too. "I am honored."

"And as for your dear wife, Cite. Klemp, we need help in the laundry. She looks strong and willing to work."

"I'm certain that will be fine. For both of us." Josiah's heart skipped a beat at the assumption he could—and would—speak for Julia. But then again, they were married. "Do we start tomorrow?"

"Yes. I will introduce you to Cit. Bromme before you leave tonight, and he will give you instructions. Cite. McDonald will advise your wife on her duties."

Perhaps one of the women gathered around Julia right now was just such. Marie gripped her new mama's hand and stared up at each woman in turn, brow pulled down and head tilted to one side as she absorbed the strangeness of her new surroundings.

He understood exactly how she felt.

After arranging the chairs, colonists sat and waited, chatting amongst themselves. Unsure if a hierarchy existed for seating, Josiah and Julia held back. But within a few minutes, several couples beckoned they arrange themselves beside them.

A tall, spare woman approached the lectern and set a thick book on it. "Good evening. I am your speaker for tonight." She caught Josiah's gaze and then Julia's. "Welcome to the Klemps, our newest *citoyens*. My name is Cite. Marchand." She waited while several seated nearby patted them on the shoulder or nodded in their direction. "Tonight, I will read from the Bible." She flipped to her section. "In English." A man next to Josiah groaned, apparently preferring another language. "For the benefit of our newcomers."

Josiah gripped his daughter's hand as she nestled between them and steeled himself for the reading. A dribble of perspiration trickled down his back, and he wriggled his shoulders to relieve the itch.

Marie squeezed his hand and glared at him. "No fidgeting, Papa."

He bit back a smile at her so-grown-up words. "Sorry."

Julia pursed her lips and motioned for his silence as well. He sighed. Now he had two women governing his every word and action.

As well as a board of leaders in the colony.

He forced his mind back to the woman at the front of the room. Her words, spoken in a musical lilt with a faint hint of

85

French, began with a story he'd heard a time or two before. About a woman caught in adultery. John eight, according to Mrs. Marchand. If he recalled correctly, Jesus let her go with just a warning.

Probably why the tale never sat well with him.

After all, if there was no punishment for sin, why resist at all?

What was the point?

~ ~ ~

Julia's breath caught in her throat at the words read by Cite. Marchand. How was her situation so different from the woman caught in the arms of her lover? Certainly, she had no intention of consummating this mock marriage, but who would believe her protests? After all, wasn't the goal to convince the colonists that they were married not only in name but in every way? Nobody need know Marie wasn't her biological daughter.

Woman, where are those thine accusers? Hath no man condemned thee?

She perked up and pulled her thoughts back to the reading. What next?

No man, Lord.

Neither do I condemn thee. Go, and sin no more.

86

Cite. Marchand closed the book and stepped down. A minute or two of silence followed the reading, then rustling of skirts and shuffling of feet indicated the meeting's end.

Julia, however, remained glued to her chair. What did that mean? Go and sin no more. So far as she knew, she was a good person. Perhaps a little hasty with her curt responses, but not much beyond. She'd had no complaints about her bedside manner. Gotten along with her colleagues. Josiah hadn't complained or corrected her. Which was just as well. She wasn't certain how she'd react if he did. No matter their marital status.

Was somebody—God or an astute citizen—trying to tell her she needed to change her behavior? Was her bogus marital situation so evident that God—or whoever—felt the need to shout her lie to the entire community? And if so, was this the way they handled discipline all the time? Through shame and humiliation?

Except the French Icarians claimed no religious beliefs. Entirely secular as regards the running of the commune. Each free to pursue—or not—their own theology. These evening reading sessions weren't a substitute for church, but an opportunity for residents to gather and relax. Since not all could read, the readings gave all the chance to learn. Tomorrow, the piece could be from a newspaper, a favorite novel, or a treatise on naval warfare.

In English, French, or any of the other represented languages.

At least, that's what Cite. Marchand told her.

Marie tugged her hand. "Mama, time to leave."

Josiah stood. "I will meet with Cit. Bromme to discuss my duties for tomorrow. Have you received your instructions?"

"Yes." Although not thrilled with her assignment as junior laundress, no doubt under the supervision of a harried woman with a short temper, blending in was important. She could not raise any suspicions by revealing her medical training. "I begin after breakfast." She turned to Marie. "And you will attend school."

Marie's brow dropped. "But I don't want—"

Josiah patted her head. "We must do what's expected of us, at least for the time being, my sweet."

Cit. Marchand strode toward them. "It pleased us you attended this evening. Are you settled in?"

Josiah nodded. "Yes, thank you."

"Cit. Bromme will meet you outside. For now, we must extinguish the candles, then exit."

Julia led the way, with Marie and Josiah following like dutiful chicks in her wake. Once outside, she stood to one side with Marie while Josiah discussed arrangements for his leather and harness making work.

While waiting, she chatted with Marie, encouraging her about school. "You are very intelligent. The other children will see that and will like you."

"I've heard there are different levels. Will I start at the first?"

Julia smiled. "They are called grades. The teacher might give you a test to see where you'd best fit. However, since this school meets in one schoolhouse, you'll soon move into a seat in the best grade for you. And I will help you in the evenings with any extra work so you quickly catch up with the children of your own age." How much to share with the child? "I actually skipped the third grade because I could read so well."

Marie's countenance brightened, and a smile eased the worry wrinkles on her forehead. Surely this child had taken on responsibilities and experienced situations far beyond her years. Giving her hope and resources to succeed would be her immediate goal. Time and plenty of feminine attention were the prescription of this doctor.

Josiah joined them, and together they headed for their log cabin home.

And then, tomorrow—well, she'd worry about that when the sun rose.

~ ~ ~

By the time they arrived home, Josiah's leg and back ached so that he collapsed on the bed, still wearing his clothes and boots. Julia and Marie busied themselves with the remaining small details of getting their little home in order, including cleaning cobwebs from the corners. He kept his eyes clamped shut, hoping they'd think he slept so they wouldn't ask for his help.

When Marie bumped the bed, he opened one eye. The child, flushed from her exertions, apologized. "Sorry, Papa. I was trying to hurry because Mama said I could go outside and play if I finished early."

He grunted and turned on his side. But inside, joy rose in him at his daughter's simple acceptance of Julia as her mother. While she most likely remembered the woman who birthed her, not mentioning her name or allowing discussion of her communicated volumes about how they must both forget her. To speak of her would surely open old wounds and reveal information best forgotten.

Julia called from the other side of the room. "Marie, you may go now."

Marie propped the broom near the door. "Thank you, Mama."

Josiah closed his eyes again as the cabin fell silent, apart from the sounds of Julia rinsing a washcloth, the droplets of water falling into the basin, splashing and spattering like rain. Then her skirts rustled. Swishing as she addressed the grime on the sideboard. More rinsing.

He groaned. No rest for the weary was surely true. He'd best get up and —

A ruckus outside drew his attention. A scream—his daughter's, for he'd know that tone anywhere—pierced his soul, and he hurried to the door as fast as his gimpy leg and stiff back could carry him.

Through a palisade of legs, he glimpsed his daughter and exhaled. Marie knelt on the ground beside another child. As he neared, Julia pushed past, her face white. Several other youngsters and teens formed a ring around the one on the ground.

Out of breath, Josiah eased and wriggled his way into the circle until he stood at a child's feet. A boy. About Marie's age.

91

A Gauvain boy, if he recalled from the introductions earlier today. Gasping for air, his feet rooted to the ground, he reached for his daughter and pulled her to his side. She clung to him, her shoulders heaving.

"Oh, Papa, it was horrible. August dared us to climb that tree." She pointed to a large cottonwood beside the path through town. "He got so high up, we couldn't see him. Then he cried out and fell, hitting his head."

Guilt overwhelmed Josiah over his relief that the injured child wasn't his own. What would he do if Marie lay there, face white as death, blood seeping into the dry ground? Nothing. He'd do exactly what he always did. He couldn't kneel like Julia did. He couldn't run for help.

But he could pray. He dropped his chin to his chest. *Father, please help this boy. Don't take him from us at such a tender age. Jesus healed all who came to Him.*

He lifted his head. Julia pressed her ear to the boy's chest, then to his mouth. Checking for breathing. Then she ran her hands over his body, beginning with his shoulders, arms, chest, legs. Finally, she felt around the back of his neck, moving his head from side to side in tiny increments, her eyes glued on the boy's face.

She looked up at those gathered around. "Somebody run and tell his parents he's hurt. And you—" She pointed to a teen girl. One of the Marchands. "Tell your mother I need something for bandages. And a heavy curved needle. And thread. And scissors." She caught his eye. "Hot water. Boiling if you can get it."

He nodded. He'd go to the sun and back for what she asked. All she need do was speak the words.

He held Marie's face between his hands and brushed away her tears. "Do you want to come with me or stay?"

The child looked back at the boy, then gripped his hand. "I'll help you, Papa."

Together, they hurried into their cabin. She fetched a pail of water while he lit the stove. Their abode would be like an oven tonight, but saving a child was worth the discomfort. Once the fire blazed, he poured water into the coffee pot, heating it in small batches to make the process go quicker. After each pot came to the boil, he poured it into the jug used with the washbasin. Three repetitions, and the container was full.

He pointed to the wash cabinet. "Get as many towels as you can find in there."

Marie located four lengths of muslin used to dry their hands

93

and faces, and they headed for the scene of the accident. He set the bowl down, and his daughter stood by, towels ready to hand off to Julia.

Her forehead shone with perspiration despite the cool night air. Her mouth, pinched as she focused on the task, gave him new insight into her abilities. Of course, he knew she was not a clerk in a mercantile. Her demeanor proved she was beyond that work. Her manners and accent defined her as something more than a servant, and her vocabulary demonstrated education far beyond his own. Perhaps even college.

She turned the boy on his side and examined the back of his head. "He's got a nasty gash." She pressed a cloth to wound. When blood soaked through within seconds, her eyes widened, and her brow pulled down. Another cloth. Then another.

She shook her head. "The only way to stop the bleeding is to stitch him up." She looked around at the onlookers. The activity had attracted several adults. "Is his mother here?"

Cite. Gauvain stepped forward, wringing her hands together. "Is he alive?" She clasped hands to her face and wailed. "Oh, God, don't take my baby."

Julia touched the woman's forearm. "Will you give permission for me to try to save him?"

Josiah stared. What kind of question was that? What parent wouldn't grant such authority in a heartbeat? Granted, she didn't know these people well, but why would she think perhaps the mother wouldn't agree?

Cite. Gauvain's head snapped up. "Can you save him?"

"I can but try. But I cannot guarantee it."

The mother clapped her hand over Julia's where it still rested on her arm. "Do whatever it takes."

Julia nodded once. Short. Brisk. Like a period on the end of a sentence. "Please hold him like this." She showed where his mother should grip his shoulder and support his head. "He might feel the needle, so prepare yourself to hold him still."

The second girl appeared with the stitching tools, setting them on the ground in a bowl. Julia poured a dollop of the boiling water into the container, letting it set while she dabbed at the wound with a damp cloth. After tossing out the water, she threaded the needle as if she'd done so a thousand times before. Was she a seamstress? A dressmaker? That would explain her ease at the idea of sewing up a wound. And spending time with those who could afford her services no doubt was the source of her proper manners and educated speech.

Then she sat back on her heels and rested her hands in her

lap.

His breath caught in his throat.

Was she too late? Had the boy died?

Another tsunami of fear threatened to wash him off his feet as he considered the ramifications.

If he had, what would that outcome mean to their staying here?

~ ~ ~

Julia breathed in and out through her nose, eyes closed as she sought to block out those gathered around her. Goodness, she'd done far more complicated surgeries than this in the past. Hundreds of times. No, thousands. She'd not been this nervous on her very first assist with Dr. Thatcher at the medical college for women.

Then again, less rode on her performance for that resetting of a broken leg than this simple suturing of a scalp laceration. Dr. Thatcher had stood beside her then, ready to take over should something go wrong.

Here, she was on her own. No wonder she trembled like a newborn kitten in a snowstorm.

"Julia?"

She opened her eyes at Josiah's voice. One she'd know even

better in the months and years to come. Until the day she left, of course.

She tossed him a half-smile, then one to the boy's mother. "Ready?"

"Y-y-yes."

Not exactly the vote of confidence she sought, but it would have to do for now. A deep breath.

Steady, hands.

She inserted the needle that looked better suited for stitching leather than a child's skin through hair and blood. Her earlier examination proved that only the outer epidermis had torn, the jagged contours suggesting his contact with a tree branch rather than the hard ground. Which was good news. Landing on his head might have splintered or cracked the cranium, leading to a worse prognosis. As it was, this wound proved easier to treat, and the boy should have a speedy recovery.

Still, she wouldn't get ahead of herself and make promises over which she had no control.

She'd learned her lesson in Des Moines.

Julia bent over her work, focusing on gently pulling the thread through and tying off each stitch. What she wouldn't give for a proper pair of forceps, some laudanum to dull the boy's pain, and surgical thread. Still, this should do. And once healed, should be practically invisible beneath the boy's hair.

She must be doing something right, since the boy whimpered but once, quickly settled again by his mother's calm whispers. If only all parents could constrain themselves once the initial shock abated.

After about fifteen minutes, Julia straightened and dropped her tools into the bowl. She dabbed at her forehead, cheeks, and neck with a clean cloth. Perspiration dribbled down her spine, tickling and itching at the same time. But the boy rested quietly. So far, so good.

Using a length of bandage, she wrapped his head round and round, attaching the end with a pin, waiting to ensure the bleeding stopped. Once satisfied, she looked up at the now-sizable crowd watching her every movement. "Can a couple of you men carry him on a board or a door to his bed?" She turned to his mother. "You've been very brave. Let him sleep where it's warm. In his own bed, if you can. Keep him quiet for a few days. He may have a headache or an upset tummy. That's normal. Try to get him to take liquids. Let him use the night pot. He shouldn't walk for at least two days. I'll stop by and check the wound tomorrow. Our chief worry is infection."

His mother nodded her understanding, then eased her son onto the door brought to carry him to their home.

Julia shrugged back her shoulders, easing achy muscles. Funny how exhaustion could clash with such invigoration at the same time.

Success did that, she supposed.

A hand entered her peripheral vision. She looked up. Josiah. She slipped her hand into his as he assisted her to a standing position. The ground beneath her feet wobbled—or was that her knees?

She stared into his eyes, seeing something she'd not noticed before.

He knew.

Exactly what, she wasn't certain.

But in saving this boy's life, she'd perhaps ended her own opportunity for a new start.

Chapter 7

From the chair near the stove in their cabin, Josiah listened as Julia read a bedtime story to Marie. Not just any story. The same one. Over and over. Because they owned just the one book. No, they actually owned several, but he'd forced her to choose just one when they fled their home two years before.

Reading by candlelight, any worry lines on Julia's face vanished. Whether that resulted from the flickering flame or the activity, he wasn't certain. But mothering agreed with her.

Several minutes later, Julia closed the book. "Enough of

Cousin Grace for tonight. Your eyes are heavier than thunderclouds.''

"Goodnight, Mama." She blew a kiss in his direction. "Nighty-night, Papa. Sleep tight."

"Don't let the bedbugs bite."

His rejoinder brought a smile to her lips as it always did. Their traditional goodnight closing always tickled his daughter. If only he could always keep things happy for her.

But life wasn't like that. Not for him, anyway. Not for Marie.

And probably not for Julia, either.

She crossed the room and lifted the coffee pot. "Would you like a cup?"

"You have beans?"

"Yes, a wedding gift from Mr. Bacon. A full pound of his best." She hefted a small canvas sack tied with a drawstring. "Shall we sit outside for a time?"

He glanced at his daughter. Her even breathing indicated that, as with most children, she'd fallen easily into slumber. What about young Gauvain? Would he sleep as easily tonight? Or would nightmares of his fall disturb him? Perhaps the young were more resilient. He wished he was. Nightmares of the war still woke him regularly.

But the opportunity to get to know this puzzling woman better was too good to miss. He nodded. "Yes, that sounds good."

A few minutes later, the smoky-bitter scent of coffee burbled from the pot. Julia poured them each a mug, then headed for the front door. He rearranged a couple of half-barrels for them to perch on, deciding that proper chairs were next on his list of projects when he had time away from the harness shop.

After they settled, she wrapped her hands around her mug as if warding off the evening chill.

"Are you cold?"

"No, it feels good to be out here. The cabin is a little warm."

"Yes. We can blame the fire today for that. I suspect we'll be glad when winter comes that it heats so quickly and holds the warmth well."

"Yes. The winter." She stared into the night and sipped her coffee before speaking again. "It's been a strange day."

"A lot has happened since rising this morning."

She chuckled. "Not exactly how I envisioned my wedding

day."

He leaned forward, elbows on his knees. Her words reminded him of how different his marriage to Sonja had been. Open. Comfortable. Full of hope and dreams for the years ahead. Until she changed after Marie's birth. Became mean, irritable, cruel. "Do you regret your decision?"

"N-n-o-o."

He chuckled and settled back. "Good. I'm glad you're certain."

"Oh, I didn't say that."

His heart thudded, threatening to burst out of his ribcage. "You're not sure?"

She sighed, one shoulder lifting, then falling back into place. "I think we've made the best of a bad situation." She leaned forward, laying a hand on his forearm. "I really appreciate what you've done for me."

What did she think he'd accomplished? Convinced her to hide away with him in a communal colony. Where they'd never own their home. He could never afford to buy her something nice. Where they depended on the kindness of strangers to provide their basic needs.

And despite her words, she was the one who'd sacrificed far

more for him. For Marie. She could have gone anywhere. Lived a life of relative ease. Found a husband to love and cherish her. Have a family of her own.

Not a borrowed one, like his.

He peered through the gloom into her eyes, trying to read the hidden depths. So why had she agreed to his proposition? What secret did she hide? Nothing criminal, of that he felt certain. A husband already? A bad marriage, perhaps? Yes, that was it. She'd married a lout. One who drank or gambled—or both—all their money. Perhaps threatened her life. Sought her. Which was why she leaped at the offer of this pretend marriage.

Perhaps neither was being honest. With the other. With themselves.

He waved off her words. "We are helping each other. We'll not speak of it again."

She snatched back her hand as though he'd bitten her. Strange. Wasn't that what they'd agreed to? A marriage in name only? That was all he could offer her.

"Very well. If that's what you want."

His mouth turned down in a half-frown. "It's best if we don't discuss this. For Marie's sake. For the sake of the colony." He met her gaze. "Someday we'll tell our grandchildren about this day, and they won't believe us."

His statement hung between them like a wet blanket, and he wished he could snatch back his words. Of course, he meant the offspring from a future relationship with another. Not each other. What right did he have mentioning grandchildren? She'd stay until Marie could look after the household. Four or five years. Maybe six at most.

And then she'd leave.

An elephant sat on his chest, threatening to cut off his breathing. He'd known this woman all of three days. Why should the thought of her moving on pain him so much? Not since the shrapnel pierced his back and leg had he felt such excruciating burning, tearing, and ripping.

Except this time, not of his flesh.

Now his heart lay in a heap, as surely as if she'd walked away, carpetbag in hand.

A desire to share himself with this woman tugged at him. But why should he open himself to her ridicule? Wouldn't that simply make her absence more difficult? Would she think he tried to convince her to stay with his sad story?

Or would she instead see his true feelings and desires for her?

The thought of her not being in his life overtook him.

If she determined to leave, perhaps—for all their sakes—she should do it before the wound became mortal. Let her leave now. He and Marie were in residence in the colony—surely they could stay even if Julia Belvedere Klemp abandoned them.

He'd take the chance and see what good God could bring from it. Didn't His Word promise that what was meant for bad would be turned to profit?

He drew a deep breath and exhaled. Best get it over with. "Forgive my presumptuous words."

"It's all right." She set her mug on the veranda. "It's just that right now I struggle to think that far ahead."

"And today is the first day I've allowed myself that luxury."

She turned to face him. "Why is that?"

"There are things about me and Marie that you don't know."

"And about me I've not told you, either."

"I met you at the lowest time in my life."

"Really? How so?"

He sipped his coffee to wet his throat. "Hmm, that's good. I'll have to remember to thank Mr. Bacon the next time I see him." Unwilling to spoil this special moment, he hesitated, then plunged in. "I'd considered killing myself so a good family could adopt Marie in Quincy."

Julia's eyes widened, but she remained silent.

"I see I shock you. It surprises me to speak of it now. I feel as though I'm telling another's tale. But truth is, if I'd identified a family that would take her, my plans included a rope and a high beam in the livery barn."

She reached across the space between them, stopping short of making contact. "I'm so sorry circumstances brought you to that point."

He waved off her words. "Such thoughts flew out the window when I met you. Your words of encouragement caused me to hope that things could be different. I never envisioned we'd come to an understanding in this way."

She nodded. "But that's all it is, right? An understanding. To help both of us out of a difficult situation."

He quirked his head toward the interior of the cabin. "You get along well with Marie."

"She is easy to like."

"And you handled yourself well today with the injured boy." He waited a couple of heartbeats, and when she didn't respond, he pressed in. "Almost as if you'd done it before."

Her shoulders stiffened, and she turned her body away just a little, as though putting distance between them. Had he pushed too hard?

He chuckled to relieve the tension in the air. "I wondered if you were a seamstress or a dressmaker. You handled the needle and thread as if born to it."

Her jaw worked, and she opened her mouth to speak, not once but thrice, clamping her lips shut each time. Much like earlier, as she worked on the boy. He'd keep an eye out for that signal, or, as the gamblers said, that *tell.*

Not that he knew much about gamblers.

No, that lifestyle was just about as foreign to him as being both father and mother to his daughter proved two years ago.

But despite the hardships and the uncertainty, he couldn't stay with Sonja. Not once he learned the truth about her treatment of Marie. From all appearances, a loving mother and wife. Unfortunately, not only to him, but to every man who could fog a mirror. A truth he learned on his return from the war. No longer hale and hearty, depressed by his change in fortunes, he'd languished around the house.

Which was how he discovered his wife's ongoing infidelities.

And when confronted, she blamed him. Implying he was no

longer man enough.

That's when he learned the truth. Even before he went off to defend their freedom and way of life, she'd frolicked—and more—with multiple men. To the point, he wondered about his daughter's paternity.

Well, that concern lasted about as long as an eye blink. Marie was his daughter, through and through.

When he discovered bruises on the little girl's arms and legs and learned about beatings from both her mother and the men she entertained, he could tolerate the woman's behavior no longer. It was one thing to torment him day and night with her infidelity. He would not tolerate mistreatment of his daughter.

So perhaps Julia's plans to leave would prove beneficial.

Not only was their marriage a sham on the surface, but in reality.

He was still married to Sonja.

A good thing, perhaps, for Julia.

It made leaving easier.

So why wasn't his heart assuaged?

~ ~ ~

How much did he know? Or did he merely fish for the truth about her? Perhaps he wasn't who he said, but somebody sent to return her for prosecution to Des Moines.

She highly doubted this possibility. In fact, she was fairly certain this man held as many secrets—if not more—than she. Still, he'd shared *some* of his story—if what he said was true, that is.

The words she longed to speak caught in her throat, and she hesitated, still uncertain how much to say. If anything. Perhaps now was the time to remain silent. Otherwise, he might think she sought to one-up him in the sad tale department.

But if he expected a response, what could she say? She barely knew the man and knew even less about what he needed.

Eye-to-eye contact was key. As was avoidance of any discussion regarding her medical skills. She swiveled to face him, her heart clanging against her ribcage. When did what he thought or wanted begin to matter so much to her? Surely she couldn't be developing feelings for this man. Could she?

She swallowed back her fear like a chunk of unchewed meat. "I'm just glad I was here to help. The boy's mother helped to calm him and me. And everybody was so helpful and kind."

He peered at her, his brow low, mouth pursed. She hadn't fooled him. Now she must be extra-careful to hide her true calling. Once she could explain away, perhaps, but a pattern of medicining would soon draw too much attention.

Josiah Klemp was an intelligent man. One not to be trifled with when it came to hiding anything.

She offered a smile, hoping to dispel the stiffness in his shoulders. Or maybe that was merely his tired and aching back.

He nodded once, then stood. "Time to retire for the night."

Her chest tightened. Sleep. Bed. Heat rushed to her cheeks. Why hadn't they thought to discuss their sleeping arrangements before now? She couldn't—wouldn't—lay in the same bed with him. And although Marie was but ten years old, she'd still expect to see her Mama and Papa together in the morning. Particularly tonight. Her wedding day.

She groaned. When had life become so complicated?

A slow smile crept up Josiah's face, as though he read her mind. He gestured to the wooden stoop. "I will sleep out here tonight."

"But Marie—"

"Is innocent of the ways of husbands and wives. We have been—uh, she has been without a mother for several years. What she might have observed is probably long forgotten. And if she asks, we will tell her my stomach was in turmoil over the excitement of the day, and I didn't want to disturb your sleep."

Her breathing slowed. "You are most gracious. Although I could say I wasn't feeling well."

A brisk shake of his head decided the matter. "It's my responsibility."

Her new husband sleeping outside might work for a short time. But their wedding night? Already she feared the repercussions. Neighbors would talk, raising questions they didn't want to answer.

"And tomorrow night?"

"We shall arrange something else. Perhaps a bolster down the middle of the bed once she is asleep."

Perhaps something between them—other than their pasts—would work.

~ ~ ~

The next morning, Josiah clambered to his feet as the sun peeked over the rolling hills surrounding the community. Best to rise before the neighbors so he didn't have to answer awkward questions. After brushing dust from his britches and folding up the two quilts used for bedding, he eased into the house, blinking until his eyes adjusted.

A glance at his daughter's bed area confirmed she still slept, her face peaceful in slumber. Julia sat on the edge of the bed, already dressed, twisting and pinning her hair into a graceful concoction of loops and curls.

He set the quilts on the foot of the bed, then nodded in her direction. "Should I make coffee?"

Pink colored her cheeks, whether from pleasure or embarrassment at being caught during her daily preparations. He'd love to know which. A revelation that startled him. Would she stick around long enough for him to discern the difference?

"That sounds marvelous." She tucked the final comb into place, then stood, brushing out her skirt. "I was told yesterday that I would receive work clothes at the laundry today. I'll be glad not to have to wear this same dress every day."

"I'll also receive a homespun shirt and something called denim britches. The seamstresses tailor clothing for the entire community."

The memory of her skill with a needle and thread still haunted him, as did the fact she avoided his observation on the matter. Perhaps he could mention to Cit. Marchand that his wife's abilities lay in that area rather than the laundry.

After lighting a fire with kindling, he set the coffeepot on the stove and added beans. Next he extracted the basin and jug from the cabinet and set both on the wash surface, poured

115

water into the bowl, and washed his face and hands. "Ooh, that's cold."

"Good. I thought perhaps I was being overdramatic when I washed up last night." The color in her cheeks deepened at the mention of her personal hygiene. "I'm sorry, that didn't sound kind. I didn't mean I was glad it was cold. I meant—"

He chuckled and soaped his face, then addressed his beard with a straight razor. "I understand." He rinsed the blade and quirked his chin toward Marie. "Time for her to rise, too. We don't want to be late for breakfast."

"Of course. I'll do that in a moment."

As he completed shaving, Julia's tender words the previous day to his—their—daughter reminded him how gentle she was. He normally bellowed from the other end of the wagon or nudged her pillow to awaken her.

He could get used to this.

As could Marie, he reckoned.

He rinsed off the remaining lather and ran his fingers through his hair. T'would have to be good enough.

As he peered at his reflection in the wavy mirror, his rumbling stomach complained of the many hours since supper, although yesterday's meal proved more than he'd eaten in any one day for a long time. According to the information conveyed by Cit. Marchand yesterday, breakfast was light, dinner at noonday being the largest meal of the day.

He perched on the chair and laced up his boots while Julia nudged Marie's shoulder and whispered something into the child's ear. He smiled when his—their—daughter pulled the covers over her face, but Julia persisted, peeling back the blanket and tickling her under the chin.

With a loud groan, Marie flung off the quilt then shuffled off to the privy at the rear of the cabin, returning a few minutes later, still rubbing sleep from her eyes. She climbed up on his lap and snuggled against his chest, playing with a button on his shirt.

He ruffled her hair. "Time to dress for breakfast. But first, wash your hands and face." When she protested, he tickled her, sending her into fits of laughter. These moments of not worrying about where their next meal would come from freed both of them to enjoy each other's company. But... "Up you get. Perhaps Julia would dress your hair today."

Marie poked a forefinger into his chest. "Not Julia. Mama." She wriggled out of his grip and scurried to Julia's place on the bed. "Would you, Mama?"

Josiah bit back laughter at his wife's widened eyes and raised brows. Such panic over a little girl's pigtails. He couldn't leave her in such a state. "Two braids for your first day of school?"

Marie considered the offer, then nodded. "So long as they hang down the front."

"Why's that?"

"So, if there's a boy sitting behind me, he can't tug them or dip them in the ink bottle."

He pulled his mouth down in a mock frown. "And where did you learn that?"

The child planted her hands on her hips. "The other girls told me." She glanced up at Julia. "Is it true, Mama?"

His wife's bottom lip tremored. "Sometimes boys can be really mean."

"Why?"

"Well, at your age, because they like to tease. Later on, when you're older, it can mean they like you."

"I don't like to be teased. And if they like me, why not just say it?"

Julia's shoulders shook with mirth. "That's a good question. And yes, I'll braid your hair. But first, as your papa said, wash up." She quirked her chin toward the cups awaiting filling, then turned back to Marie. "Where is your comb?"

"Under my pillow."

After enjoying their cup of coffee while the girls giggled over Julia's attempts to fix Marie's hair, they left their cabin after passing each other's inspection. It pleased him they all wanted to put their best foot forward on this first official day in the community.

After a short walk to the refectory, they gathered with the other residents on the grassy area, greeting one another and passing the time until the doors opened. Names eluded him, so he simply smiled and nodded. Julia stood at his side, her arm looped through his, greeting several women by name, then pointing out their husbands for his benefit. Marie played with the other children.

Cite. Gauvain arrived her gaggle of children in her wake, slowing and nodding to Julia. "Thank you for saving my boy. He is feeling so much better already. Says he has no headache, but he is hungry."

Julia smiled. "That's good news. If he continues in this manner, you may bring him tomorrow."

"He'll be pleased to hear that."

The refectory door opened, and Cit. Marchand stepped out,

joined by another man. When the crowd quieted, he addressed them. "This is Wesley Richard. Please give him whatever help you can. He seeks a woman fugitive from Iowa. A Doctor Brown."

Julia gripped his forearm so tight he thought she might break the bone. He turned his head to ask her to relent, but her reaction stole his words. Color drained from her face, and she froze like a statue. Or a deer caught in a hunter's lantern light.

Interesting. What about this man would cause this reaction?

Did she know the person he sought?

Or was she acquainted with him?

And if so, professionally?

Or personally?

~ ~ ~

Julia sank onto the edge of the bed in her shared cabin, head pounding like a stampede of angry bovines. This time, the headache she claimed was real, and slipping away from breakfast proved simple.

She massaged her temples, ears alert for the sound of footsteps running toward her. Of the door bursting open, and a man with a badge—and likely a firearm pointed at her—hauling her back to face a trial and hanging in Des Moines.

Her stomach tossed and roiled as she considered her situation. How had he tracked her down so quickly? She shouldn't have stayed. She shouldn't have connected with people. Got a job.

Gotten married and fallen in love with both father and daughter.

Then again, she'd traveled as far as her meager resources could carry her. Done what she could to avoid detection: changed her name. Forsook medical work. Accepted a position beneath even a first-year student.

Except some things she had little control over. Her physical appearance. Mannerisms.

Inability to refuse to treat a wounded boy.

Would her Good Samaritan actions reveal her identity and be her downfall?

She stood and paced the floor, skirts swishing around her ankles. What to do? What to do? She'd rather face a lacerated artery than this decision. In the surgical case, life was always the preferable choice to death.

In her situation, death was the only option. If she stayed, they'd convict her of medical manslaughter. If she ran, she would leave behind everybody she cared about, and along with them, her dreams of a second chance.

She paused. Maybe she could convince Josiah and Marie to come with her. No. They'd settled in well. Josiah seemed happier, and Marie already blossomed under the family love and communal care of the other residents in the few hours since they arrived. She couldn't yank the child's first stable home in two years out from beneath her.

Their peace and comfort mattered to her. While uncertain how Josiah felt about her, Marie wore her heart on her sleeve. Just this morning, as she braided the little girl's hair, enjoying the silky touch between her fingers, Marie felt compelled to give her a lesson in understanding her father. With him sitting there, listening to every word. The ache in her chest eased as she recalled the child's words.

"Don't worry if he stomps out and won't talk to you. I've learned he isn't angry with me, but disappointed in himself. So don't pester him. Leave him be."

Was that but an hour ago? Hard to believe that world of innocence existed alongside the mountain of troubles she now faced.

She stared out the window. Breakfast would soon be over. By then, the Pinkerton man would have talked with all the residents and garnered what they knew. No doubt at least one would mention the Gauvain boy's fall and her ministrations. He'd soon put two and two together and come up with the right answer.

She spotted her carpetbag beneath the bed. Did she dare make a run for it? Hide out in the woods until he gave up and moved on? And if he did, what then? Would she live the rest of her life always looking over her shoulder?

Josiah's Bible on the table caught her eye. If only she had faith enough to believe God might intercede for her. Just this once. Perhaps if she promised to stay and be the best wife—in every way—to Josiah that she could, He'd help her out. Just this once.

At this point, she had nothing to lose by asking.

She lowered herself to her knees beside the bed, uncertain where to begin. "God, it's me. I know we haven't been on speaking terms in the past, but there's something I need right now. Some might call it a miracle."

~ ~ ~

Josiah slowed as he neared the house, hefting his bundle of work clothes under one arm. Julia's voice carried out the open window next to the door.

"I love Josiah and Marie with all my heart. And maybe that's a miracle You've already granted. But now I need another. Please tell me what to do. Should I stay? Or go? I'll do anything if You let me stay. I'll be a real wife for Josiah, and a real mother for Marie. I'll work hard here at the settlement. Please, God, let me stay. Thank you, God. Amen."

After her hasty departure from the refectory yard, claiming a sudden severe headache, he'd found himself distracted several times while eating and conversing with other residents. Once or twice, he asked a tablemate to repeat themselves, and even Marie peered up at him, her dark eyes large and solemn.

What was Julia talking about? Staying or leaving? Why did she think that choice was necessary? Was she unhappy with them? In this place? Thankful Marie wasn't present to hear her mother's words, he hesitated. Should he barge in and insist she explain herself? Or pretend he'd not overheard her prayer and wait for her to explain?

And what did she mean, she'd do anything? Including being a real wife—his cheeks burned at the implication of her words. To the world, she was truly married to him. What would he do if she insisted on consummating their marriage? Could he resist her? Then what would she think of him? Perhaps if he denied her the physical intimacies she believed important to her bargain with the Lord, she'd think him less a man.

After speaking with the Pinkerton agent at table, Josiah sought to put together his suspicions, the lawman's description of the woman doctor, and Julia's expertise at medicining the boy. He shook his head. What a fool he'd been, attributing her skill to that of a seamstress.

With Marie sitting beside him while eating, he'd not felt comfortable asking more probing questions. However, after exiting the building and seeing her off with a group of other children, he gathered with Cit. Bromme and two other workers in a corner of the yard.

After receiving their instructions for the day, and he his work attire, talk turned to the stranger in their community. Cit. Bromme filled in additional information shared at a meeting of the leadership prior to breakfast. "Agent Richard seeks this woman regarding a medical malpractice case. A boy died while under her care. That was all he could say until he speaks with the doctor." He shook his head and shuffled his feet. "It is a sad day when a child dies." He caught Josiah's eye. "Perhaps your wife missed her calling. We hear she saved August's life."

Josiah stammered past the lump in his throat. "I-I-I don't

think she'd say that. Sh-sh-she staunched the blood and stitched the wound."

Cit. Bromme peered at him beneath bushy eyebrows. "Perhaps she should work on the leather, and you could do laundry." Josiah and the other two remained silent. Then Cit. Bromme clapped him on the shoulder. "Just pulling your leg."

Uncertain of the meaning of the statement, Josiah stared at his boots. "No, both legs are in the proper position."

Bromme laughed. "I mean, I am jesting. Your job is secure in the harness shop, so long as you learn quickly and are willing to work."

Still not convinced which path to take regarding Julia, he stepped onto the stoop. He wouldn't confront her with his thoughts on her identity. If he did, she'd likely feel pressured to leave, which would break his heart. And Marie's.

For now, he'd stay silent. Pretend he hadn't overheard her.

And do what he should have done before now.

Trust God to work all things together for good, just as His word promised.

Then again, didn't He also say that the truth would set him free?

Perhaps now was the time to experience that freedom.

Before either of them did something they'd later regret.

Chapter 8

The next day, as Julia and her little not-quite-genuine family headed to the Refectory for breakfast, she overheard the Marchands ahead of them discussing the same topic two of the younger girls bantered between them the previous day at the laundry. Seemed the entire community wanted more information about the frequent meetings of the Leadership that were conducted behind closed doors. Cit. Marchand, one of the five overseers, shook his head several times, no doubt refusing to tell his wife more than was permissible. It appeared nobody outside that group knew the topic, just that the hush-hush meetings began when the Pinkerton agent arrived in town.

However, apart from the individual decision of each citoyen and citoyenne on whether to assist his investigations, the Leadership—as far as she could gather—constrained themselves from dictating behavior unless it negatively affected the community. Thankfully, the residents maintained order through mutual care and respect, rather than a long list of do's and don'ts. If a decision benefited the colony, folks tolerated it. If not, Leadership made a visit.

Still, she'd keep her ears open. With too much to lose if this Agent Richard poked his nose into her business, she could ill-afford him uncovering her subterfuge.

She paused inside the door, so abruptly that Marie and then Josiah bumped into her. She turned and tossed both a half-smile in apology. "Sorry. It's so bright outside that I stopped to let my eyes adjust."

Marie scooted past her and waved to a friend. "See you later, Mama."

The child hurried to sit beside the girl, their heads instantly close as they whispered and giggled. Josiah stood beside her, their shoulders touching in the narrow hallway.

He placed a hand on the small of her back. "Children make friends so easily."

She forced herself to relax under his touch. "Yes. Such a blessing."

He glanced at her. "I think so, too. I wish I could do the same."

She faced him, so close his breath warmed her forehead. "You do a wonderful job of meeting people, of fitting in, despite—" Her cheeks colored. "I mean—"

He held up a hand. "I know what you mean. But I must work diligently to overcome my desire to shrink into a corner and stay silent. The effort to mingle exhausts me more than the physical movement."

Her heart sank into her toes. She'd not given a moment's thought to his pain or disability, instead seeing the strong man and the loving father inside. Had his spirit shriveled along with his limbs? She pressed against his touch. "I'm sorry. I didn't know."

"I've learned to disguise both my physical pain and my predilection for solitude."

Interesting words. Josiah was no ignorant laborer. He sounded like a man of some education. "I'd like to discuss that some evening. Differences in personalities, and how we each cope, since we seem to be so different."

He nodded, a smile lighting his face and erasing the care from around his eyes. "I'd like that, too."

She surveyed the room. "Do you want to join another table, or shall we sit alone?"

His brow raised at her suggestion. "Alone, I believe. I'm still recovering from the chatter at the leather shop yesterday."

She'd enjoyed her time at the laundry, to her surprise. The two assistant laundresses knew everybody, although Julia wondered if they had all their facts correct. Still, through their chatter, she'd vicariously met residents she'd not been formally introduced to yet. And heard of adventures and scrapes of several, although she'd not decided yet how close to the truth the tales trod. Despite the hot and hard work, she returned home in the evening with enough energy to sweep the cabin, then read two stories—or rather the same story twice—to Marie before the child's bedtime.

At a nearby table, one family joined hands and bent their heads in prayer. Interesting how the colony kept a purely secular model of government, yet allowed folks of all faiths to take part privately as they felt led. The nearest town, Quincy, nine miles away by wagon, boasted the only church in the area. That distance could prove prohibitive in poor weather, but perhaps the family made the journey on Sundays. Might she be bold enough to ask? If so, why? She had no faith of her own, yet recent experiences had pushed the limits of her beliefs. She wished she had someone other than herself—and maybe Josiah—to lean on.

Now *that* might be another topic of conversation they could engage in another evening. Something—anything—rather than their personal situations and plans to keep up appearances.

When Agent Richard entered the room and joined the Marchands at their table, conversation around the room quieted for about three heartbeats—or a little more in Julia's case— before resuming, although the subject abruptly changed from his presence to the upcoming harvest. Apparently, a party happened later this month that included inviting folks from town to share in the joy and bounty. A tradition of the colony, where the kitchen cooked for days, and everybody else contributed through labor to clean and paint and help the community put its best foot forward.

After breakfast, she hugged Marie, who turned up her cheek for the Continental kiss—one on each cheek—before hurrying to catch up with her school chums. Josiah stood beside her, shuffling his feet in the dirt. She hesitated, uncertain how to handle their separation for the day. Yesterday was simple. One of his co-workers grabbed his attention, and he left her side without even a backward glance. However, after checking the behavior of the other couples, she concluded that if they repeated that lack of familiarity too often, they'd draw questions.

Best to nip suspicions in the bud.

She leaned close and touched his cheek with hers, first the left, then the right, without making lip contact. "Enjoy your day, Josiah."

His eyes widened at her gesture, then a slow smile lifted the corners of his lips. How she longed to lean closer and touch them with hers. Were they soft yet firm as they appeared? Then the memory of his dead wife intruded, and the magic of the moment fled. Voices converged and the other residents appeared in her periphery, each intent on beginning their work.

She pivoted and headed for the laundry, nodding to several she knew along the way. Once inside, she lined up behind the other three girls and women, awaiting her assignment for the day.

Cite. McDonald—all of four feet eight—smiled up at her. "Greetings. You did good work yesterday, despite it being your first day."

"Thank you." The others sought the woman's praise, as they'd shared with her. And rarely received it. "I appreciated your clear instructions."

"And I like it when folks listen." She scanned her list for the day. "Bedding from the east cabins will arrive shortly, along with the towels from the bath house. And this afternoon, personal clothing from the west cabins."

Julia sighed. Eighty families' worth of items. Several dozen shirts and dresses and skirts and blouses and pants for ironing. Some might even require additional scrubbing, particularly the children's clothing.

A full day's work, to be sure.

"I have assigned the others to inside work. Perhaps you'd enjoy working outside? You can rinse the items in the tub, wring them out, and hang them."

That might prove pleasant. The day promised moderate temperatures with a quick drying breeze and warm sunlight.

She nodded. "Thank you."

In fact, as she'd observed the previous day, whether or not she'd have chosen the task made little difference to Cite. McDonald. The tone of suggestion, however, made an unpleasant task more bearable.

Two hours later, Julia wondered why she'd thought this assignment might be the better. She labored over the enormous iron pot, stirring the sheets in water hot enough to scald, fueled by the fire beneath. Despite the use of lye soap, Cite. McDonald insisted on the hot rinse. Apparently her horror of bedbugs and lice drove her to these superhuman efforts to eradicate every singly pestilence possible.

She swiped the sweat from her forehead. Several drops dribbled down her face and dropped to the rim of the cauldron, dancing and sizzling on the hot surface. She straightened and addressed the items waiting in the now-tepid but previously cold-water final rinse tank. Already her hands, chapped and raw from the work, stung as she pulled out a sheet and wrung the water back into the receptacle.

Oh, to be a man. Sitting in the coolness of the leather room, cutting, stitching, molding. Perhaps even able to use creative ability to etch a piece into a piece of art. Men had it so easy.

She repeated the process with another sheet, then bundled both into a basket and headed for the drying lines up over a rise. Already six lengths of muslin flapped in the breeze, most likely ready for removal.

She trudged up the incline, head down, watching for gopher holes as she went. She'd learned that lesson yesterday, too, when she stepped into a burrow, almost twisting her ankle. An injury like that might prove cause to be asked to leave, and that wouldn't do.

When she topped the rise, she set the basket down and surveyed the valley below, pressing her knuckles into the small of her back. The land below—belonging to the colony for as far as the eye could see—rolled in fields of wheat, corn, and oats. And just over there, toward the schoolhouse, the remains of strawberry fields, now past production, as well as potatoes, beets, cabbage, and carrots.

Using a hand to shade her eyes, she allowed herself one more moment of upright stature, purposely pressing her shoulders back to ease the ache building. How did Josiah manage his pain, day in and day out? She'd seen him wince and grimace at movement that irritated, such as picking up his daughter when she ran to greet him. Or when bringing in an armload of wood for the stove at night. And when he rose in the morning, stiff from inactivity and chill.

Yet he never complained. Never railed at Providence or whatever he believed in.

Movement below caught her eye. The Pinkerton man. She stepped behind the line holding the sheets, peering through the gap between them. His horse loped along as though neither had a particular destination in mind. Just looking.

For her.

Although he didn't know it.

Yet.

Without warning, his brown gelding reared and pawed the air, neighing and snorting as though startled. Strange. She saw nothing. The man dug his heels into the stirrups and tightened the reins, but the horse persisted. When its front legs finally reconnected with the earth, now its back end came up.

Having overcompensated to stay seated, Agent Richard went over the horse's head. The gelding gave a final buck and moved about twenty feet away before dropping its head to nibble at the grass, its tail flicking at flies as if nothing else in the world mattered.

Julia muffled her laughter with a hand, not wanting to give away the fact she'd seen him fall. In her experience, men hated looking foolish. He'd rise, dust himself off, perhaps toss a curse at the retreating beast, slap his leg with his hat, then walk to the colony for another mount.

Instead, he remained prone. Unmoving.

Her heart raced. Did he know she watched? If so, did he wait to entrap her?

Or was he seriously injured?

Perhaps dead.

Well, if the latter, that certainly solved her dilemma, for the short term, at any rate. Of course, another would come to take his place, but perhaps by that time, she'd have drummed up enough courage to take her leave.

The doctor within her warred with the fugitive. Help him or leave him? Assist or ignore?

The doctor won.

She gathered her skirts in one hand and trotted down the rise to where the man lay. His white face told her he wasn't faking the situation. She dropped to her knees and first checked his neck. Not broken, thank goodness. Unlike the Gauvain child, no obvious gash on his head. She slid her flattened hand beneath him, feeling for injuries. Or blood.

Her hands probed a knot where he'd hit a rock with the back of his head. However, the contact hadn't broken the skin. Perhaps he'd simply knocked the wind out of himself?

A rattling in the calf-high grass caught her attention, and she froze. A rattlesnake, its diamond markings unmistakable, coiled near his feet, tail raised, warning her away.

She groped at his side in search of a weapon. Nothing. Inside his coat? She located a two-shot gun inside a jacket pocket. Gripping it with both hands, she pointed it at the snake and took a couple of deep breaths. With only two bullets, her aim must be accurate.

Bang!

The snake flinched and thrashed its body but recovered quickly, merely injured. It raised its head, poised to strike what lay nearest—Agent Richard's leg. Perhaps for the second time.

The urgency to kill the snake and treat the Pinkerton man for a possible venomous snakebite gave her a resolve and strength she'd not known she possessed. She fired again, this time blasting the snake's head clean off its body, which quivered twice, then lay still.

She swiveled to the agent's torso and ripped open his shirt, checking for the telltale fang marks. Nothing. Now to check his legs. Heat flamed at her cheeks. How to do so with modesty and decorum? After all, if the man wasn't unconscious, how might he react if he awoke and found her peeling off his clothes? There had to be a better way.

She'd start with removing his boots and rolling up the cuffs of his britches.

Her hands trembling and her breaths gasping, she began with the left foot. Thankfully, where the boot ended, just below the knee, she found what she'd hoped she wouldn't. At least her discovery meant she'd not have to remove any more clothing.

Two triangular-shaped injection sites where the slithery creature made contact, perhaps when he fell. Had he remained astride, he'd be safely down the trail.

But he hadn't. And with no other course of treatment available, she drew a breath, then placed her mouth on the wound, drawing out blood, spitting it on the ground, and repeating the process. Never having done this before, she did not know how quickly the poison might spread. Or how far. Two minutes, three, five passed.

She sat back on her feet. What next? Keep the blood flow contained as much as possible to the affected leg. If the venom reached the heart or brain, sure death. Asphyxiation would soon follow as paralysis caused the muscles to slow his breathing until he expired. In smaller prey, this enabled the snake then to consume its next meal.

After unbuckling his belt, she cinched it around his thigh

about halfway up, then she rested. She'd done what she could. Now to wait.

"Cite. Klemp, what are you doing down there? Are you injured?"

Cite. McDonald's voice carried on the afternoon breeze, pulling her from her exhaustion.

Julia stood and waved. "I'm fine, but this man isn't." Surprisingly lithe for her size and age, the head laundress trotted toward her. When close enough so they didn't need to shout, Julia raised a hand for her to stop. "Perhaps you could summon several men to carry him back to the village?"

"Yes, of course."

When the woman turned to get help, Julia sat beside her patient again. A little color had returned to his face, and his lips were less blue. His eyelids fluttered, and he moaned.

Then pale blue eyes stared up at her. He blinked. "You."

"What?"

"It's you. Julia Brown."

"No, you're wrong." The lie stuck in her throat, yet she must persist. "I don't know what you're talking about. I'm a simple laundress."

He raised his head and looked around, then sank onto the

ground. "I've seen your picture."

She stood. She hadn't considered that. A generic description of an ordinary-looking woman had been her hope.

What to do?

Her chest ached with the effort of breathing. Her brain buzzed with choices. Run. She must leave. Now. But what about Josiah and Marie? No, she must go. Staying would shatter their lives even more. Best to leave before the two really grew attached to her. Permit him to find another woman. Another wife. One more worthy of him and his love. One able to give him what he really wanted.

Backing away from the agent, her eyes never leaving his in case he sought to restrain her, she glanced over her shoulder, directing her toward his mount. Gripping the halter and speaking soothing words to the beast, she gathered her skirts, tucked her toe into the almost-too-high stirrup, then pulled herself into the saddle.

Without a backward glance, she raced away.

From the one man intent on her imprisonment and perhaps her hanging.

From the other who loved his daughter enough to offer her refuge.

From any hope of a future with a family of her own.

Away.

~ ~ ~

Where was she?

Josiah gritted his teeth against the pain in his leg and back as his borrowed horse pounded along the hard-packed dirt track leading out of town. In the two hours since receiving word of Julia's encounter with the Pinkerton agent and her subsequent stealing of his mount and heading west, his mind hadn't stopped asking that question.

Or perhaps the phrase constituted a prayer of sorts.

Since forcing his aching knees to the floor of the church, allowing him to humble himself before his Lord, peace had enveloped him.

And even learning of her fleeing the colony hadn't stolen even a moment of connection with God. Instead, empowerment filled him as he placed Marie into the care of the schoolteacher until his return. She'd assured him the child could stay as long as needed. Being one of seven children still living at home with her parents, she said another made little difference.

But honestly, he hadn't expected her race toward the Pacific Ocean to carry her so far in such a short time. Surely the

Pinkerton's horse must slow soon, else it would collapse beneath her.

And then what? Would she land safely? Or end in a heap on the ground? Against a rock? Or a tree? Injured.

Or worse.

He crested a rise and pulled his painted pony to a halt. The animal dropped its head to snatch at a tuft of grass, its sides heaving. If he intended to cover more distance, he'd best slow his pace. Already lather flecked the mare's neck and chest. No point in him becoming a victim to a downed horse, too.

From here, he surveyed the valley below and the foothills beyond. If she hid in the trees, he'd likely not spot her. But if she raced pell-mell, thinking nobody followed, he just might—

His breath hitched. Why might she believe he wouldn't come after her? That he wouldn't hunt high and low for her, no matter her reason for leaving. Why, if she asked him to go to the moon and bring back a hunk of green cheese, he would.

Certainly, they'd made an agreement regarding the form and function of their marriage. His head understood, but apparently his heart refused to adhere. And their busy life left little time for intimate conversations. In fact, she seemed intent on keeping their relationship exactly as both agreed.

But that was then, and this was now.

He'd fallen in love with Julia Belvedere Klemp.

Josiah gathered the reins in preparation for setting off again when a glint of sunlight down near the stream meandering through the valley below caught his attention. He shaded his eyes with a hand, soothing his mount with a pat on the neck. He peered through slitted eyes. Nothing.

Perhaps a reflection off the water? He lifted one shoulder, relieving the pressure from his war wound, and waited. There it was again. Definitely metal. Moving away from him.

He kneed the pinto down over the grassy hill. Leaning back into the saddle and digging his feet into the stirrups, he compensated for the steepness. At the base, he slapped the mare's hindquarters with his hat, propelling it into a gallop. Lying low over its neck, he gave the animal its head, relishing the response of racing through the belly-high grasses.

Within a couple of minutes, he'd caught up with the horse and rider. Despite the slumped shoulders, he'd know her anywhere. Her gelding turned its head as they neared, ears pricked forward but head low. Done in.

As was he. Almost.

However, the sight of the only woman in the world he

wanted to hold in his arms lifted his spirits and gave him the energy to call her name. "Julia."

She swiveled in the saddle, eyes wide. Then she kicked at her mount's sides. But as if listening to a higher power, the animal refused to move one step further, stopping instead, nose to the ground.

She kicked again, and when the beast ignored her, she slid from her perch, landing in a heap on the ground. Unhurt, she gathered her skirts and fled, leaving the horse to its own designs.

He bit back a chuckle. If she thought she could outrun him, she was wrong.

He'd crawl on hands and knees to get to her if needed.

About twenty feet from her, he reined to a halt, the pinto's back legs digging in until its hindquarters met the ground like a dog begging for a bone. He stepped out of the stirrup and onto the ground, gathering enough breath to beseech her to stop. "Wait."

She glanced behind, then turned again, apparently intent on making this far more difficult than necessary. Fine. He'd sworn to himself he'd track her down. Supposing it took until the beaches in California.

Thankfully, reaching her didn't take that far or that long. Despite his gimpy leg, he reached her in ten strides, gripping her arm and pulling her against his chest. Her legs gave out, her chest heaved against his, and he held her close, telling himself he didn't want her to fall.

Sure.

And even once she'd regained her breath and wriggled her hands up, planting them against his now sweat-dampened shirt, he held on.

As if for dear life.

Which it was.

His.

~ ~ ~

"What?"

Had she died and gone to heaven? Surely only that would explain how the man who'd stolen her heart could sit here telling her the news she'd longed and prayed for.

Julia stared at him. "You mean—"

He nodded, then leaned against the trunk of the cottonwood they sat beneath. Nearby, their horses nuzzled each other, tails flicking in the shade of another tree. "I wouldn't lie."

Of course, he wouldn't. Josiah Klemp would rather bite off

his tongue than lie. So why had his cheeks ruddied at that statement? As if his statement embarrassed him. Interesting.

"So, tell me again. I think my brain only caught every other word."

"Agent Richard came here looking for a woman doctor from Des Moines. He believes you're that woman."

She held her breath. Best to hear him out completely.

"He passed out when the men lifted him onto the board to carry him into a house, but regained consciousness shortly after. Thankfully, he proved lucid enough to pass along his message. In fact, thanks to your ministrations, he sat up and drank a cup of tea less than an hour later. You saved his life, which he well acknowledges."

The knot between her shoulders eased a mite. "I'm glad he appears on the mend."

Josiah nodded. "Once again, you were exactly where somebody needed you." He smiled, the expression softening the wrinkles around his eyes and taking ten years off his face. "Something you seem to make a habit."

She squirmed under his gaze and the meaning behind his words. What could she say? To dismiss them would prove nothing. Best to hold her counsel.

"Julia, before I tell you the rest, there is something else we must speak of."

She exhaled. So, this is how it would end. Her hopes and dreams of a haven dashed against the rocky ground like a fine china cup smashed on a rock. Had she really thought anything good could be possible for her? That she might simply walk away from her past and into a new future with this fine man? That might happen in fairy tales. Or romance novels.

But not in her life.

Not to somebody who others said made such a heinous mistake as to cause the death of a child.

How could she expect him to trust her with Marie once he knew the truth?

She wouldn't, given the reverse situation.

She clasped her hands in her lap, tying her fingers into knots.

What could he possibly tell her she didn't already know? How he wanted her to leave them be? Then why would he chase her down? Hadn't she set out to do exactly that?

Letting her go, thinking she decided for them both, would have been far kinder.

This—this was cruel.

And Josiah Klemp was anything but cruel.

He drew a deep breath, then exhaled. "Our marriage is a sham."

Well, she knew that already, didn't she? Wasn't that their agreement? Wed for the child and for propriety, nothing else. Certainly not for companionship.

Definitely not for love.

"I am already married."

Interesting turn of phrase. Not *I was already married.* That was obvious. He had a daughter, and presumably, she had a mother at some point. *I am married.*

She tilted her head to one side. "As in currently?"

He hung his head until his chin touched his chest. "Yes."

Apparently, she didn't know him as well as she thought. He did lie.

As if she had room to talk. Her entire life had become one huge untruth, far beyond the bounds of white lies or fibs.

"Continue."

"Her mother was a kind and loving woman when we wed. But something happened after Marie's birth. She turned melancholy. Mean. Short-tempered. Not just with the child, but with me, too."

Julia nodded. "That happens sometimes. We don't understand its cause yet, but there have been several studies with disparate outcomes and recommendations for treatment."

"I mentioned it to our doctor, who said she was simply overwhelmed. I tried to do more at home, but she refused my help. Her reasoning was unsound, but when I stopped, she then blamed me for lying about the house doing nothing, even after I'd worked twelve to fourteen hours a day. I hated going home, although I desperately missed my daughter." He exhaled. "I didn't miss my wife. She was already gone, as though dead to me."

An ache filled her chest and worked its way up her throat. So, that was that. She'd fallen in love with a married man. Pretended to be his wife. Loved his daughter, too, as though from her own flesh. Now what?

Her fingers stilled in their weaving, then clenched into fists. She should smack him until he begged for relief, that's what. Perhaps add a judicious kick for good measure. He didn't deserve her. Or her love.

She froze. Goodness, what if she'd confessed her feelings for him? Spoken the words aloud, unable to snatch them back and cram them into the hidden recesses of her mind?

Would he laugh at her naivety? Mock her for believing him? Ruin her good name throughout the colony as a bigamist?

No, the Josiah Klemp she knew would never.

Which just proved how little she actually knew of his true self.

He touched her hand, drawing her back. "I stayed until I discovered marks on Maria's back and legs. The child admitted her fear of her mother, who'd beaten her for burning her toast that morning. I couldn't allow my wife to mistreat my daughter. We left that day and have been running ever since." He held her gaze. "I'm sorry I lied to you. But I thought that if—when you learned the truth, perhaps by then Marie and I could manage on our own, far enough from my wife that she'd never locate us."

"You thought it would make it easier for me to leave."

"Yes."

His words hung in the air between them as final as a judge's gavel pronouncing sentence.

She'd been correct all along.

He didn't want her.

~ ~ ~

Josiah waited for a response. Anything. Crying. Screaming. Flailing out at him. Continuing her ride westward.

153

All of which he deserved.

But not this silence. Deep as the ocean. Dark as a moonless night. Convicting as a hangman's noose.

Before she left—or forever cut him from her life—he must deliver the good news he carried. Good for her, that is. Because if she still needed a reason to leave, this would be it. Her freedom. A pardon so she could continue her life.

He licked his dry lips, wishing he drank alcohol. And had some handy. But he didn't. To either. "Agent Richard asked me to deliver a message to you. I don't understand everything, but he said to tell you the medical board exonerated you completely. They dropped all charges. The father admitted the child was sick for five days. He didn't want to spend the money to bring the boy in until it was too late." He paused for a breath. "Does this change things for you?"

Color returned to her face, and her entire body relaxed as though easing into a feather bed after a long day's work. Good news, to be certain. For which he would rejoice with her.

"Yes."

The single word, barely above a whisper, carried much weight.

Which now transferred to his heart.

Seemed that good news for her meant bad for him.

Chapter 9

As she and Josiah returned to Icaria, Julia pondered her good luck. No longer did she need to continue living a lie. She could now choose her future as a free woman.

She glanced at Josiah, riding beside her, teeth gritted. He'd risked permanent damage by coming after her. If the shrapnel in his back worked its way into a vital organ, perhaps slicing through an artery, he could die. Had he considered the possible injury to himself? Had he decided the risk worth the reward?

Perhaps she'd been wrong about him. If he didn't want the love-and-cherish-until-death-did-them-part bit, he at least still needed her to continue his disguise. To protect his daughter from his deranged wife. And to care for—and hopefully still love—Marie.

Best to get the truth into the open. Now. When she could keep her eyes on the road ahead. On the space between her mount's ears. On the brass buckle on the bridle. On anything other than the layers of her heart, which cracked and tore, ripped asunder, at the reality of her situation.

She'd fallen in love with this man and his daughter. She didn't want to leave. She longed to stay with them, to continue to call themselves a family. But only if he truly wanted her.

The Pinkerton agent's words, instead of tearing down her world, instead ruptured her fears. She could be a doctor again, treating the sick and injured. She could be Doctor Julia Brown, not simply Mrs. Josiah Klemp.

So why did that realization hurt so much? It's not like she'd had any fairy tale ending in mind regarding her and the crippled harness maker. Their story would instead be a tragedy, woven from threads of deception and lies, at least to the world. And perhaps to themselves, as well.

They'd live the rest of their lives looking over their shoulders for a crazy woman intent on dismantling their carefully constructed house of cards to snatch back a child unable to protect or defend herself. And what could Josiah do to stop her?

Well, he'd already taken the drastic step of snatching the child from her mother and disappearing into the vast west of the country. And then he'd jumped at the opportunity to encase them in a communal society here in Icaria, hoping his marriage would throw off anybody coming in search of them.

She groaned within. Her attempt at the same subterfuge had lasted all of about a week, even changing her name, family status, and occupation. The Pinkerton man still found her.

She cleared her throat and pulled back on the reins before swiveling to address Josiah. "We need to talk."

"Y-yes." His voice croaked as though he'd inhaled a hundred miles of dust instead of merely ten. "I'm sure you have many decisions to make."

"Not only that." She exhaled. "About Marie. I'd like to examine her on our return."

"Of course."

"And if I concur with your allegations, contact the sheriff. Tell him what has happened. Surely there is legal recourse available to protect your daughter from abuse."

His shoulders slumped. "I'm afraid they won't do anything,

but that her mother will find us. And take her back."

She picked up her reins again. "Let's cross that bridge when we get to it."

Satisfied she had a plan in place, she nudged her mount.

Easy for her. This wasn't her daughter she risked losing.

~ ~ ~

Easy for her. It's not her daughter.

Josiah worried over the plan Julia concocted, certain she sought a way out of their fake marriage. Why didn't she simply leave? She had no reason to stay, not after hearing what the Pinkerton man said. And his own. Even if they both wished otherwise, Julia was no bigamist. Yet her words indicated her intent to stay for the short term, at least.

And then? Then he and Marie would do what they'd done for the past couple of years. Get along. Now in a much better situation, thanks to the Icarians. For the first time, Marie laughed. Played with children her own age. Formed friendships. Perhaps, in time, he'd follow her example.

Just not yet. Not while his heart wept for what might have been in another lifetime. Another world.

He closed his eyes, blinking back tears that threatened to overflow. *God, if You can, please fix this mess I've gotten myself into.*

He stared ahead, wishing he and his daughter could ride off into the distance. Into a future without fear. Without scars.

One that included Julia.

Because right now, that's the only happy ending he could conjure.

~ ~ ~

In their log cabin, Julia stared at the scars laid across the child's arms like a crisscross pattern. She'd seen marks like this but once before—on the hindquarters of a draft pony sorely abused by its owner for not being able to haul an overloaded freight wagon out of a foot-thick mire of mud.

In that case, the lout wielded a leather whip as a weapon.

But in this?

A shudder passed through her, and she stifled a moan emanating from deep inside. Who would do this to a child? Josiah contended his wife had. If true, then the question became why.

She patted Marie's shoulder. "You can pull your sleeves down, now." As the child complied, Julia jotted notes on a makeshift medical chart which she'd created from a sheet of stationery a resident donated. "Are there other marks?"

"Yes." The child kept her chin tucked under, her voice low.

"On my back."

Interesting that as crazy as the girl's mother might be, she injured her daughter in places where the marks were less likely to be seen. Arms easily covered by sleeves. The back, hidden under clothing.

"Would you be willing to show me those as well?"

Marie turned away from her and undid the buttons running down the front of her dress, then slipped the thin cotton material over her shoulders, exposing her back while clutching her dress modestly to her chest.

This time Julia couldn't control her reaction. Her breath caught in her throat, and her hand went to her throat. Welts similar to the ones she'd already seen marred the tender skin. And interspersed, round blemishes with raised edges dotted this unholy canvas.

She ran a finger over one, noting the child's tremor beneath her touch.

Burns.

But with what?

"You may pull up your dress again, Marie. Thank you for trusting me."

The girl turned to face her. "Of course, I trust you. You're my mama."

The words tore at Julia's heart anew. No, she wasn't really her mother. She was simply her papa's wife.

But the terrible truth was that her real mama did this to her.

Yet the child trusted *her*.

She didn't deserve that. Particularly since that faith would rupture when she left.

At a knock at the door, she pushed aside her thoughts, brushed her skirt, and turned the record of Marie's injuries upside down on the table. Then she smiled at the girl. "Would you mind watering the flowers for me?"

All signs of the child's worries disappeared, replaced by a wide grin. "Of course, Mama."

Once the child exited through the rear of the cabin, Julia answered the door. On the front step stood Cit. Marchand, hat in hand.

"Good evening, sir."

"I am here on behalf of the Leadership of the community."

Julia stifled a groan. Surely no good ever came of an introduction of that sort. "Did you want to speak with Josiah? He isn't here right now."

"No, it's you with whom I wish to speak."

162

Oh, dear. What have I done this time?

Perhaps the Pinkerton man reported to them, and they'd decided she was not a suitable candidate for the settlement.

Well, that made her decision easier, at least.

She stepped back from the door. "Come in."

He entered, shoulders broad, back straight. So unlike Josiah physically. Yet, she had no doubt the man she called husband—even if not truly so—was equal to this imposing figure in every way she found important.

He sat on the chair near the unlit stove, twirling his hat by the brim. She perched on the bed and waited. No point in hurrying bad news.

After a moment, he cleared his throat. "We understand you are a medical doctor."

Ah, so the detective told them. "That's right."

"From what we've seen, you are very good. You could earn a good living elsewhere."

Was that her invitation to leave?

If so, why did his words hurt so much?

She nodded, her fingers worrying at a button on her cuff. "I could."

"So you'll be leaving?"

Why couldn't the man simply voice what needed saying? Must she pull everything from him like extracting a tooth? "Is that what you want?"

He blinked several times. "No. We prefer you remain." He smiled. "The cabin next door is vacant. We hoped perhaps you'd find that convenient to set up a medical office."

A medical office? Here in Icaria? "You want me to practice medicine here?"

"You are a doctor. And as you can see, we need occasional medical expertise." Another twirl of his hat, like a period on the end of his statement. "Would you consider staying?"

With most of her reasons for leaving resolved by the Pinkerton agent's news, remaining in Icaria could be an option.

She stood. "Thank you. I will."

For now.

~ ~ ~

Josiah sat in the remaining empty chair on the front step later that evening. The sun disappeared several hours before, and his daughter slept peacefully in her bed. Julia occupied the other chair, still and quiet in the near-darkness.

Time to talk.

"You examined Marie?"

The chair creaked as Julia shifted to face him. "I did. You are correct. She has been abused. Severely. Practically tortured. And she told me the same." Silence for a long moment. Would she continue? "You were right to remove her from the situation." Another pause. "I understand your concerns about speaking with the authorities."

"You saw for yourself how unfairly they treated you. And you did what you thought best in leaving Des Moines."

"Yes. The family was furious. They were upstanding citizens. And I but a woman. Whose son died at my hand, or so they thought."

"The law isn't always right. I was so afraid that I could think of nothing else than to run and hide."

"And now?"

"Nothing has changed for us."

"Yet nobody has come asking about her. Or you."

"Hopefully, I've run far enough." But was that even possible? Perhaps not until he stood on the furthest spit of land, might he feel safe. "And if not…"

His words hung in the air between them. Not a threat, but a promise.

He'd leave here in an instant to save his child.

~ ~ ~

If he left with his daughter, would he take her with them?

Oh, please God, let him say so.

When he didn't complete the sentence, she sighed. While pretending marriage with her to gain access to this community proved expedient, he'd likely not encumber himself in his flight westward. Now that she could be a doctor again, her skills would draw attention to their family situation, no matter where they went. He'd likely prefer anonymity.

Footsteps crunched away from their cabin, and she held her breath. Who'd overheard their conversation? She'd not heard anybody approach.

She drew a deep breath. "Who is there? Announce yourself."

Josiah stood. "Can you see them?"

She peered through the darkness, wishing she'd thought to bring a lantern. "No. Who do you think it was?"

"No idea. And why they didn't reveal themselves is a mystery." He limped back to his chair. "It worries me, though."

"Surely you don't think your wife has spies here?"

"I wouldn't put it past her. She is an evil, vindictive woman." He stood again and offered her his hand. "Come. We

166

must retire."

Inside, she rolled the quilt into a long tube, changed into her nightclothes while Josiah kindled a slow-burning fire to ward off the chilly evening, and crawled into bed, pulling the bolster beside her. So far, they'd arisen in the morning before Marie awoke, straightening the quilt over the bed, thus averting questions from the child.

So far.

But if the girl awoke during the night, she might notice something amiss.

And then answers would be required.

But as her own mother used to tell her, time enough to worry about that when it happened. For now, each day had enough troubles.

Tomorrow, she'd begin setting up the cabin next door. Cit. Marchand assured her that colonists would construct whatever she needed. They'd order anything else from a catalog.

She wasn't so certain.

A peaceful heart and a happy family weren't built or purchased.

~ ~ ~

The next morning, Julia swept the empty cabin free of dust and spider webs. Already stacked outside were several chairs, donated for the waiting area. She chuckled. As if she'd have so many patients as to need even one. Later today, carpenters would arrive to build a couple of partition walls separating the public space from the treatment areas. Imagine, two rooms to see patients. As well as a small corner where she'd store and complete paperwork. Order supplies. Catch her breath.

The wood stove stood near the front door, ready to produce heat and hot water as needed. She'd already insisted on two single beds in one treatment room. One for an overnight patient, and the other in case she needed to watch over that person. Or if an expectant mother needed a place to give birth.

She paused and leaned on the broom, studying dust motes dancing in beams of sunlight streaming in through the now-clean window. Curtains, yes. Next on her list. And a tank for water. Several residents promised old sheets for bandages. She'd incorporate Marie's help in the evenings, tearing the material into several widths, then boiling them to ensure their cleanliness.

Josiah stepped inside and surveyed the area, smiling. "I see you have all well in hand."

"I do. Thank you."

"Is there anything I might contribute to your office?"

"Perhaps some leather straps for braces?" She held out a hand to demonstrate. "To wrap around a sprained wrist, reaching from elbow to here." She pointed to a spot near the base of her fingers. "With a hole where the thumb could stick through, allowing the use of the digits while the carpus heals."

His brow furrowed. "Carpus?"

She giggled. "Sorry. Medical term for wrist."

He snorted. "Doctors always want to make everything more complicated, don't they?"

"It's not intentional. We train in the scientific terminology. It's a different language, that's certain, but more precise and universally understood. At least, amongst doctors."

"Might you also want a similar leather bit for the ankle or foot?"

"Oh, that would be wonderful." At the sound of footsteps on the stoop, she turned. "Sorry, we're not open—oh."

Agent Richard stood in the doorway. "I'm not here to see you, Doctor." He nodded to Josiah. "It's Mr. Klemp I seek."

Julia set the broom aside. "I'll leave you two to your conversation."

Josiah stopped her by reaching for her forearm. "Please stay.

I have no secrets from my wife."

That might be true, except she wasn't his wife, was she?

Still, she stopped and waited. Whatever the man had to say affected both of them. Regardless of their true marital state, they were in this lie together.

The detective shuffled his toe on the floor and kept his eyes on his boots. "Truth is, I overheard your discussion last night."

Josiah peered at the man. "Why didn't you identify yourself when we called?"

"Honestly, I didn't want you to think ill of me for eavesdropping. But your words caused me to consider your situation. As I returned to my room, an idea came to mind."

Seemed the man knew their deepest and darkest secrets. What did he plan to do with that information? "And what conclusion did you draw?"

"That you sounded like folks who had gotten a raw deal along the way. I wanted to help."

Oh, no. If he'd contacted the authorities back east, alerted Josiah's wife of his whereabouts...

"I had a colleague look into Mr. Klemp's situation." He held up a hand to stop her protest. "Discreet enquiries, trust me. And I believe my news will cheer you."

Josiah closed his eyes and exhaled. "Go ahead."

"I confirmed that your first wife died six months ago."

~ ~ ~

The agent's words hit Josiah like a brick. Stunned, his knees threatened to buckle beneath him, and he stumbled to one side before catching himself.

Agent Richard frowned. "I'm sorry. I thought you knew. Else your current marriage…" He paused. "You didn't know. Which means—I understand. You both were hiding here under cover, so to speak." He chuckled. "Well, you've certainly fooled everybody here. Even training the child to call you Mama."

"I—I didn't." Julia's pale countenance mirrored his own incredulity at the agent's news. "She thinks of me as such."

"I see." He glanced from him to Julia and back again. "Does this news please you?"

What could he say to this near-stranger in front of Julia? He knew how she felt. If given the opportunity, she'd skedaddle in an instant. After all, they had based their lives on protecting the child—and him—from a woman they now knew was dead.

He drew a breath, praying for wisdom. "I simply hope she found repentance before passing."

He glanced at Julia to gauge her reaction. Her bottom lip

171

trembled, her cheeks still pale.

As unreadable as a newspaper printed on black paper.

His heart sank to the toes of his boots, threatening to fracture.

He wanted her to stay.

Not just for Marie.

For him.

Chapter 10

Two days later, Josiah straggled behind the other men at the end of the day. Pain in his back had hindered him all day, slowing his movements and stiffening his muscles. He sighed. Had a piece of shrapnel worked its way loose?

Or is this how a broken heart felt?

Since learning of the Pinkerton man's information, he and Julia navigated through their days—and their nights—as if dancing a complicated waltz. Never quite connecting, never speaking of their new reality, but smiling through the ordeal for everybody else's sake.

Thankfully, Agent Richard left town yesterday, and none of the leadership mentioned the man's extra-curricular investigation, so hopefully that news would not spread through the community like a prairie wildfire.

He turned in at their shared log cabin—he couldn't bring himself to call it their home—then entered after scraping his boots on the step. Inside, the area appeared as tidy as always. Of course, they spent few hours here, primarily for sleeping, so their occupation of the dwelling made little mess.

Julia looked up from where she sat near the stove, bent over what looked like one of Marie's school outfits. "You look tired."

"Yes. But mostly from—" No, he wouldn't admit the pain. Even if she left tomorrow, he wanted her last memories of him to be good. "How was your day?"

She set the dress aside and stood. "Good. I tended to an older resident with gout. Recommended she reduce her intake of red meat, but I think she'll ignore me." She chuckled and smoother her skirts. "I stitched a boy nipped by his pet rooster and patched up a dog that wrestled with a pig and lost."

"Goodness, you're working on animals, too?"

She nodded. "All were pets, and, as the child reminded me,

they are family, too."

"I suppose."

He sank onto the foot of the bed, longing to collapse back on the mattress. But dinner was soon, so he settled for scooting back and leaning against the wall. In doing so, he twisted his back. A stabbing pain shot through his torso, and he bit back a gasp.

Julia's brow pulled down. "What is it?"

He shook his head, generating another spasm. "N-nothing."

The room spun, and dark spots appeared at the periphery of his vision. Unable to hold himself upright any longer, he slid to his right, his breaths shallow as he sought to outlast the agony.

The mattress sagged as Julia sat beside him, although he couldn't see her face. Now he worried her, though, of that he was certain.

Her chilled hand felt his forehead, and she tsk-tsked. "Can you stand to come to my office? I'll help you."

Sure, he could do that.

But the effort to raise his body from the mattress proved more than he could summon.

Bile rose in his throat, and his eyes closed.

God, protect Julia and Marie, should I perish.

~ ~ ~

Julia swiped the perspiration from her forehead as she glanced at Josiah's expression. Seemed he still enjoyed unconsciousness as she probed into the muscles of his back for yet another piece of shrapnel. Three slivers lay in a kidney-bowl at her elbow, and one remained beneath his clavicle. Perhaps she should stitch him up, turn him over, and attempt its extraction from the front...

No, there.

Her deft forefinger located the errant piece, and she trained her forceps into the channel between bone, muscle, and tendon, gripping the edge, and easing out the brass cartridge casing which troubled him. After dropping it in the dish to join its fellows, she dabbed at the open wound, ensuring she'd not nicked a vein or artery, then commenced stitching the layers of muscle together. Thankfully, she'd identified the cause of his sudden onset of pain as the shrapnel received during the War Between the States, suspecting the metal pieces moved suddenly, slicing through muscle and irritating nerve endings as it did. She'd taken an enormous risk operating on him in less-than-ideal conditions—on the bed they shared—but when he passed out, he left her little choice.

She straightened, pressing knuckles into the small of her back, easing the tight muscles, before resuming sewing the skin together with precise stitches. A sprinkling of sulfur powder, then several layers of bandage before a final wrap around his chest—her cheeks heated at her intimate view of his body.

She shook off her silliness. A patient. Nothing more. Nothing less. She'd extend diligent care to any man, woman, or child in a similar situation.

Except this wasn't the same.

This particular man held her heart captive. Clasped in his hands like a new-laid egg.

Awaiting his decision whether to protect or crush.

Which would he choose?

~ ~ ~

A week later, a knock at the door roused Josiah from his slumber. At Julia's insistence and the leadership's approval, he'd lazed around for the past seven days, his only pain the mending of skin and muscles.

"Praise the Lord."

Every time he thought of the two years of agony he'd endured since his injury, and the joy of movement now with mere tenderness as his only companion, he couldn't hold back the words of thanks to his God. After examining him this morning, Julia pronounced him fit for work, and said she'd mention to Cit. Marchand so he could resume scheduling.

When he bid his unknown visitor enter, the very man stepped inside. "Greetings, Cit. Klemp. How fare thee?"

"Well, thank you." Josiah swung his legs over the side of the bed as Julia taught him—log roll, she'd called it, saying the movement put less stress on the back than his typical practice of rolling onto his back and sitting up—then straightened the quilt. "And you?"

"Fine. Fine. They have missed you at the harness shop."

Josiah forced a smile he didn't quite feel. Grateful for any opportunity to provide for his family, the tasks of sewing and repairing weren't exactly—well, manly. And more than anything, he longed to prove to Julia he could be the man she needed.

And wanted.

Particularly now that he was free to do so.

Cit. Marchand chuckled. "Sometimes we do what doesn't make us happy in order to bless another, yes?"

"Yes. And I am thankful for the opportunity." He gestured to the chair. "Please, sit. Can I offer you coffee? And perhaps a gingerbread cookie?"

Cit. Marchand's smile widened. "Both sound good."

Josiah crossed the room and tucked another stick of wood into the fire, refilled the coffeepot, and added fresh beans. While that brewed, he set a plate on the table, peeling back the cotton cloth covering to reveal four crispy rounds. "Left from last night's supper. Cook said we could bring home a plate."

"Yes, I believe we were all so blessed."

Once the coffee boiled, Josiah poured a cup for each, then resumed his seat on the bed as the two crunched their treats. He forced himself to wash down the dessert with a mouthful of coffee. Whatever could the man be lingering for?

More bad news?

Unsure he wanted to hear it, if so, he waited. And waited.

Finally, Cit. Marchand drained his cup and set it beside the now-empty plate. "As you know, all able-bodied adults must work."

"Yes."

What else could he say?

"In the worst of situations, the work is mundane and the person ill-suited."

"Yes."

"Your good wife reports you can move without pain or

limitation to your movement." He paused. "She is an excellent surgeon and doctor, and we are very blessed to have her." His gaze met Josiah's. "The leadership committee met last night and made a decision."

"Oh."

"One we hope pleases you."

Josiah swallowed hard past the lump the size of a pumpkin in his throat.

"Cite. Klemp also extolled your other fine qualities. The fact you can read and write. Do math. Are organized. Intelligent. Experienced in clerical work." He scooted forward on his chair, elbows on his knees. "We agreed to move you from the harness shop into the administrative side of the colony. Inventory, historian, and record-keeping will be your key duties. Occasionally, perhaps teach a class about finances, so they can wisely use and invest their money should they decide to leave the colony."

Had he heard the man correctly? Time to make certain. "So, I'll basically be the bookkeeper and archivist?"

"Exactly. We've not had one person performing those duties until now, but already we've garnered you space on the upper floor of the refectory, complete with desk, chair, a filing

181

cabinet, as well as writing materials." He stood and clapped his hands once. "Good. See you at work tomorrow?"

Josiah grinned. "Absolutely. Are you certain you don't need me to start today?"

"No. The paint is still drying. In the morning will be time enough." He clapped his hat on his head. "I can see myself out."

When the door closed behind his visitor, Josiah took the man's previous seat. Such good news. A position he was definitely better suited to. One not so physically demanding. Now he could help more around the cabin if he didn't completely exhaust his limited energy during the day.

Julia would be so pleased.

~ ~ ~

Well, he's certainly pleased with himself.

From the time Julia entered the cabin an hour ago, Josiah hadn't stopped chattering on about his new job, his new responsibilities, how he was so well-suited for the position.

If she didn't know better, she'd think he was trying to convince both of them of the veracity of his statements.

But no, the leadership of the colony made the perfect decision in creating this full-time position for him. After all, he'd planned to apply for the bookkeeping position at Mr. Bacon's mercantile, but she'd beat him to it.

Or had she? He'd told her about the job when she expressed her need for employment. So why had he done that? His actions made little sense to her then, and even with the passage of the past few weeks, she'd come no closer to the truth of the matter.

Well, perhaps none of it made any difference. She could leave anytime she wanted. Maybe he put on an act to convince her to do just that. Leave. Let him stay and raise his daughter, doing a job he enjoyed. And she could do the same. Elsewhere.

While in the past she'd looked for an excuse to leave, a door to open to permit her to escape the colony, now her feet felt rooted to the floor.

Or perhaps not her feet.

Maybe her heart.

Rooted in this man and his daughter.

She could identify no other explanation for her dragging her feet these past seven days. Josiah's recovery, swift and miraculous, didn't require her presence. The town could find itself another doctor if it decided it really needed one.

No, she could pack her bag, make the nine-mile walk to

Quincy, and catch the next stage to—to where? She still had no money, although she didn't doubt but the colony would provide traveling funds. And now that the investigation cleared her of all charges, she could resume medicining anywhere. Perhaps Colorado Territory. Or California.

She wrung her hands together, eyeing her carpetbag.

Leaving would be so easy.

Staying could prove much more difficult.

Epilogue

Julia stepped into a small clearing at the outskirts of the Icarian colony the next week. She clutched in her hand a carefully penned note from Marie. *Please come to a picnic down at the old oak tree today at three p.m.*

Having discovered this invitation pinned to the door of her medical office that morning, she'd hurried through her duties, glad when the last patient left at two-thirty. After freshening up and tidying her unruly tresses, she pushed her spectacles back up her nose and headed for her assignation with Josiah's daughter.

The daughter of her own heart, to be truthful.

Perhaps the main reason she'd chosen to stay—at least for the short term—was the girl and their growing relationship. Seemed Marie sought her out at every opportunity—and now this. How thoughtful of the child to arrange a little party for just the two of—

She froze. Somebody lounged on the grass, straw hat pushed back on his head. Suspenders stark against his white shirt.

Josiah. She'd know his form anywhere.

She turned to leave, then glanced at the missive. Perhaps he'd wandered in on their picnic, unaware of his intrusion. He'd move along, and she and Marie could enjoy their time together.

She stepped behind a cottonwood, intent on staying out of his sight. Had she misunderstood the note? Perhaps the child got her days—or her times—confused? *Today. Three p.m.*

Not much room there to misinterpret the instructions.

Perhaps she could hurry him along on his way, leaving Marie and herself free for a girls' afternoon out. After all, *she* was Marie's guest. Not him.

She pondered that notion. Since he'd so exuberantly shared about his new job three days previous, they'd not spoken. Seemed there was nothing more to say. Both caught in their

187

own thoughts concerning what the future held for them. Together. Separately. She had no doubt which he preferred.

Mind made up, she resumed the path and soon reached her destination.

Summoning all her acting abilities, she gasped when she entered the clearing. "Oh, hello Josiah. Marie."

She held her breath, expecting him to make his excuses and leave. When he didn't do so immediately, she glared at him, making little motions with her head for him to exit.

He stood and tipped his head in question. "Julia?" He glanced at Marie. "Did I misunderstand your note?"

"No." She waved a hand at the blanket spread on the ground. "Please, sit, Mama."

"I'll stand, thank you." She addressed Josiah. "Was this your idea?"

"Not at all."

He held out a slip of paper. Identical to her own. She reciprocated by showing her own invitation.

Together they turned to Marie, who now gazed up at them both, smiling. "You won't sit?"

Both shook their heads. Julia's stomach flip-flopped. Had he coerced the child into this charade? If so, what other cruelty might he demonstrate?

She planted her hands on her hips. "What is going on here?"

Marie clambered to her feet, still beaming at them, holding out another piece of paper. "Here."

Josiah snatched the slip and read. Then he glanced at his daughter and read it again, this time aloud. "You are invited to the wedding of the best Papa and Mama in the world. Date to be announced, but soon. Doctor Julia and Mister Josiah Klemp."

What? Had the child lost her mind?

Josiah handed her the note. "That's what it says."

Julia accepted the paper and turned to Marie. "What is the meaning of this?"

"I came home early one day and heard you talking to that Pinkerton man. He said my first mama had died." She shuffled a toe in the grass. "I'm sorry she's dead, but I'm glad, too." She stood beside Julia. "Now you really are my real mama." She gripped her hand. "And I want you and Papa to be happy." She laid Julia's hand over his. "I know you love him. Please say yes."

Julia knelt beside the girl and pulled her close, holding her tight before releasing her. "Why do you think I love your papa?"

189

"I've seen the way you look at him. How your cheeks go pink when you catch him looking at you. How you stayed up with him when he was sick." Marie stroked Julia's shoulder. "How you love me. And how you're still here with us." She shook her head. "You wouldn't stay if you didn't love him. And me."

Another hug. "You're right, little one. I do love you."

~ ~ ~

Julia's words banged around and around his ears, deafening him.

I do love you.

Not him. She hadn't stayed for him. She'd remained in the colony because of the child.

Was that enough for him? If she stayed, could he build on that foundation?

He wasn't certain.

Moreso, he didn't know if he wanted to.

For once, could he love a woman who returned those feelings?

Or was he destined to go through life alone, for the sake of his daughter?

He could do it. He'd done it once before, leaving the girl's mother for her safety.

But did he want to?

Julia squeezed his hand. "But your papa has a say in this, too. I will stay if he wants me."

He stared at her. At the unshed tears glistening her chocolate eyes. At the eyeglasses framing her orbs like a halo around an angel. At the trembling bottom lip, awaiting his response. At those wonderful curly red tresses—surely any child of theirs would be blessed to be as lovely to gaze on as their mother.

Yet she'd not uttered those words he longed to hear.

Well, perhaps he must do so first, lay his heart out on a platter. Bare it for the sake of their future.

He planted one knee in the grass, gazed up at her, and gathered her hands into his. "Julia Belvedere, I've loved you since the moment I set eyes on you. I've seen you love my daughter, cherish her, protect her, nurture her. I've watched God work in you and through you, saving lives, including my own. Would you do me the extreme honor of marrying me? I can't promise you much, except my heart, my life, and my daughter."

His words hung between them, much like that night on the front step. Except, in this case, they shimmered with an explosive intensity. As though no matter her answer, the response would knock him flat on his back.

He waited, his breath caught in his throat. Had he messed up again? Pushed too hard? Stepped out, only to allow her time and space to crush him like a spider beneath her shoe?

His head hung and his shoulders drooped. He'd done his best. Now it was up to her.

Her shoulders sagged. "My name isn't Belvedere."

His breath hitched in his throat. What else had she not told him? "Does it matter?"

"No." At a tugging on his hands, he looked up. She smiled down at him, Marie standing close beside her, also grinning. "Yes."

Yes? Was that all she had to say?

He leaped to his feet, grabbed her by the waist, and spun her round and round. She threw her head back and laughed, her hair like flames fanning over her shoulders.

Finally, she begged him to stop so she could catch her breath. He complied, and when Marie took her place, he spun her likewise, collapsing onto the blanket.

Winded, he waited until he caught his breath. "I can see that you two will be a handful. Several, in fact."

Marie scooted beside him. "And just think, Papa, when you and Mama have more babies, you'll need all my help, too."

He wrapped an arm around her shoulders. "Oh, you've already been more help than you understand." He gestured for Julia to join them. "Happy?"

She snuggled close. "Uh-hmm. You?"

"Even more, I feel free for the first time in my life."

Julia nodded. "Free to live where we want. Work where we choose."

"And love whom we want."

She chuckled. "Truly free. Just like it says in the Bible. The Son has set us free."

If you enjoyed this story, you might also enjoy the first book in the series, *Testing Tessa*

In 1868, Tessa, a Mennonite nurse graduates from nursing school and is assigned to the Amana Colonies in Iowa because of her expertise in treating asthma and other breathing problems. As a former student at a women's medical school, she knows more than most about respiratory diseases. She's also had her fair share of heartbreak when, upon her mentor's death, she was forced to abandon her dream of becoming a doctor. Will she be able to use her skills? Or will her gender keep her from helping those who truly need her?

https://www.amazon.com/Testing-Tessa-Donna-Schlachter/dp/1943688761

About Donna:

Donna writes historical suspense under her own name, and contemporary suspense under her alter ego of Leeann Betts, and has been published more than 40 times in novellas, full-length novels, and non-fiction books. She is a member of several writing communities; facilitates a critique group; teaches writing classes; ghostwrites; edits; blogs regularly; and judges in writing contests.

Keeping in Touch

www.HiStoryThruTheAges.com Stay connected so you learn about new releases, preorders, and presales, as well as check out featured authors, book reviews, and a little corner of peace. Plus: Receive a free ebook simply for signing up for our free newsletter!

www.HiStoryThruTheAges.wordpress.com

Facebook: www.Facebook.com/DonnaschlachterAuthor

Twitter: www.Twitter.com/DonnaSchlachter

Books: Amazon: http://amzn.to/2ci5Xqq

Etsy online shop of original artwork:
https://www.etsy.com/shop/Dare2DreamUS

Reviews

You've probably heard this before, but I covet your reviews. If you enjoyed this book, share that joy with other readers like yourself. Think of it is hosting your very own book club. Or imagine yourself sitting in a café with your best friend, and you simply must share about this story.

www.ingramcontent.com/pod-product-compliance
Lightning Source LLC
Chambersburg PA
CBHW071512170626
46811CB00007B/2820